可搭配 108 課綱加深加廣選修課程

U0092557

10堂課練就
TED Talks
演講力

Give a Talk the TED Way

編著者
溫宥基

學歷：國立政治大學教育學系博士

經歷：臺北市立和平高級中學校長

審定者
車昀庭

學歷：美國賓州印第安那大學語言學博士

經歷：國立政治大學外文中心副教授

★附解析本、電子朗讀音檔 ♫

三民書局

電子朗讀音檔下載

請先輸入網址或掃描 QR code 進入「三民‧東大音檔網」
https://elearning.sanmin.com.tw/Voice/

三民東大 外文組- 英文	若有音檔相關問題，歡迎**聯絡我們** ❹ 服務時間：週一-週五，08:00-17:30 臉書粉絲專頁：<u>Sanmin English - 三民英語編輯小組</u> ❺

❶ 輸入本書書名即可找到音檔。請再依提示下載音檔。

❷ 也可點擊「英文」進入英文專區查找音檔後下載。

❸ 若無法順利下載音檔，可至「常見問題」查看相關問題。

❹ 若有音檔相關問題，請點擊「聯絡我們」，將盡快為你處理。

❺ 更多英文新知都在臉書粉絲專頁。

作者序 Preface

　　自十二年國教開展以來，萬眾矚目的焦點不外乎是新課綱推行後帶來的課程革新與活化。對英文學習者來說，終於有機會可以在正規的學校課程中修習「實用」的英文而非「考試」英文。《10 堂課練就 TED Talks 演講力》正是適合高中、技高、大專院校課程推行的一套嶄新又活化的英文學習課程。

　　許多教師及學生對 TED Talks 並不陌生，但對於要如何利用豐富的 TED Talks 演講資源進行教學與學習卻感到不知所措。因此我們設計《10 堂課練就 TED Talks 演講力》，透過十堂基礎課程，藉由教師引導以及現有的網路資源，協助學生學習用英文發表演講。「一邊看、一邊學、跟著做」是這本書的精神及架構，每堂課預計在兩小時的課堂中，藉由循序漸進的步驟協助學生練就英文簡報能力。教材中所有 TED Talks 的影片，都是在合理使用的範圍下引用，以教導讀者如何運用這些演講技巧和 TED Talks 精神，發表一場精采的演講。

　　英文有句諺語："Practice makes perfect."，但是沒有引導的胡亂式練習並不會加強學生的口說能力。《10 堂課練就 TED Talks 演講力》透過課堂小單元設計，每堂課都有不同的學習重點，課堂中的所有練習都有延續性的主題，串聯在一起並整合就可以完成一場英文演講。透過循序漸進的課程設計，我們期許教師能在新課綱中開展更多英文教學的可能性，也協助學生跨出英文口說第一步。祝福教師教學愉快、學生學習有成就感。

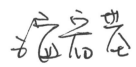

推薦序 Foreword

　　大部分看過 TED Talks 的人通常會對裡面的演講者印象深刻，因為無論國籍、口音、年齡大小，甚至談論的主題，這些演講者好像都能優游其中，泰然自若地面對觀眾侃侃而談！許多人可能心裡也都曾浮出這樣的想法：「哇！我也想要那樣說！」所以，這到底是不是一件可能的事呢？當然有可能！

　　作為學習者的我們，第一個要知道的是，他們也是練過的，而且是努力練過的！幾乎沒有人是天生的演講者，大家都得練！第二個要知道的是，練，要有方法！埋著頭自己練，常常會事倍功半，產生的挫折感可能比成就感高出好幾倍…

　　這一本書，只選擇六分鐘以內的 TED Talks 作為範本是有原因的。第一，初階的學習者也可以容易上手不害怕。第二，學習者可以看到，不用說太長也可以完整地將一個主題表達出來。而選擇這些主題來分享更有其設計上的考量。第一，是藉此將簡報中重要的技巧，利用這些影片來做示範。第二，則是因為這些主題本身能夠和學習者的生活經驗或各大議題產生連結。

　　因此，讀者可以看到全書對簡報技巧的巧妙拆解和融合，對聽說讀寫技巧的介紹與練習，包括將影片中的關鍵用語放入一篇短文中，以及一步步地教導如何檢視自己練習的成果。我不能保證跟著這本書練習完，你就會變成一個厲害的 TED Talks 演講者。但我可以保證，跟著一步步練習後，你不但會在聽力和閱讀上有所進步，同時也會對如何架構一個簡報有清楚的概念。之後，希望你再也不會對別人說：「開口說英文和做英文簡報真是令人坐立難安和恐懼啊！」

三民／東大英文教材主編

本　書　使　用　說　明

本書是專為課堂教學使用所設計的英文演講學習教材，共有 10 堂不同的主題及演講教學課程，每一課均分為 Session 1 和 Session 2 兩部分。

❶

首先 Unit 01 說明該課主題 (Topic) 和演講技巧 (Presentation Skill)。

❷

👤 **Warm-up**開始進行暖身活動，藉由圖片或表格搭配問題激發學生的學習動機。

Unit 01 — Presentation Skill · Speech Opening and Closing
How Are We to Face Death?

Session 1

👤 **Warm-up**
Discuss the following questions with your classmates.

1. What does "death" mean to you? (可複選)
   (A) A pathway to paradise.
   (B) A journey to the next life.
   (C) A route leading to nothing.
   (D) A part of the natural life cycle.
   (E) A lesson to learn that life is important.

2. If you had only one day to live, what would you do in your last moments? (可複選)
   (A) Do nothing but wait.
   (B) Spend all your money.
   (C) Follow your normal routine.
   (D) Get together with your loved ones.
   (E) Write down your final words in a will.

Watch the Video

Scan the QR code on the left to play the video.

Speaker: Matthew O'Reilly

Topic: "Am I Dying?" The Honest Answer

READING 🎧 Track-01

In the distant future, medical science may give humankind the gift of immortality. For now, though, no one can avoid death. Many people prefer not to think about the fact that one day they will **perish**. The idea fills them with **terror**, so they push it out of their mind. However, the way we think about our own death, **regardless of** our religions, could help us lead a happy life and even find **comfort** as it comes to an end.

Elizabeth Kübler-Ross spent her **career** studying the psychology of people who have been told of their imminent death. She found that their **reaction** usually follows a **pattern**. First, they find themselves unable to grasp the painful truth so they deny it exists. Then, they **respond** with anger, which in extreme cases can even lead to a violent **incident**. In the next stage, the individual's mind becomes filled with sad remembrances and past **regrets**. The final stage is **acceptance** of death. People who are dying face a **dilemma**: whether to continue the fight for life or to accept that their life will soon come to an end. After assessing their options, they usually accept the **critical** situation that they are dying. Most people are able to find **forgiveness** in their hearts in this final stage shortly prior to passing away.

While death comes to us all, we should never let our fear of death prevent us from living our life to the full. As the philosopher Immanuel Kant **observed**, "a person who is always worried about losing his life will never be able to enjoy it."

---

③ Watching the Video

掃描 QR code 就可以立即觀賞 TED Talks 演講，讓學生對本課的主題有初步的認識。若 QR code 的網址失效，請上網搜尋演講者的姓名及演講主題。

④ READING

搭配相關的 TED Talks 演講，由外籍作者編寫文章，幫助學生了解本課的主題。

⑤ 🎧 Track-01

課文和單字皆由專業的外籍錄音員錄製，增強對課文及單字的辨認能力。

⑥ 課文中的單字 Words for Production 以**粗體**標記，Words for Recognition 以彩色字體標記，加強單字記憶，並增加閱讀理解能力。

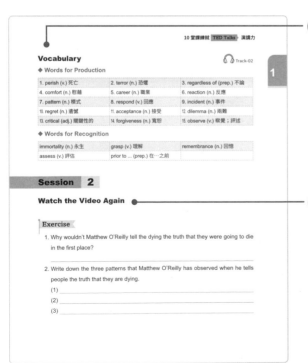

10 堂課練就 TED Talks 演講力

Vocabulary 🎧 Track-02

◆ Words for Production

1. perish (v.) 死亡	2. terror (n.) 恐懼	3. regardless of (prep.) 不論
4. comfort (n.) 慰藉	5. career (n.) 職業	6. reaction (n.) 反應
7. pattern (n.) 模式	8. respond (v.) 回應	9. incident (n.) 事件
10. regret (n.) 遺憾	11. acceptance (n.) 接受	12. dilemma (n.) 兩難
13. critical (adj.) 關鍵性的	14. forgiveness (n.) 寬恕	15. observe (v.) 察覺；評述

◆ Words for Recognition

immortality (n.) 永生	grasp (v.) 理解	remembrance (n.) 回憶
assess (v.) 評估	prior to ... (prep.) 在…之前	

Session 2

Watch the Video Again

Exercise

1. Why wouldn't Matthew O'Reilly tell the dying the truth that they were going to die in the first place?

2. Write down the three patterns that Matthew O'Reilly has observed when he tells people the truth that they are dying.
   (1) _____
   (2) _____
   (3) _____

---

⑦ Vocabulary

每課有十五個 Words for Production 及五個 Words for Recognition 單字，皆從 TED Talks 演講影片及課文中精選出來的重要單字，附詞性和中譯，強化單字學習。

⑧ Watch the Video Again

認識課文與單字後，再次觀賞 TED Talks 演講，更深入了解演講內容。

Exercise

搭配練習題，協助學生理解演講內容及細節。

9 Presentation Skill

步驟 1

跟著影片一起做 / 基本步驟 (Basics)

透過 TED Talks 演講影片，引導學生認識基本的演講技巧 (presentation skill)，每一項演講技巧後面附上於本課影片中出現的時間點，讓同學可再次複習。

步驟 2

Exercise

現學現做練習題，承「基本步驟」，馬上做練習題，提供演講時的句型 (useful expressions)，練就演講基本功。

步驟 3

更上一層樓 (Take One Step Further)

更進一步學習到延伸性演講技巧，提供演講時需要注意的事項及技巧，奠定紮實的演講功力。

步驟 4

Exercise

學會「更上一層樓」的演講技巧後，讓學生再進一步延伸，搭配練習題，提供實用的句型 (useful expressions)，加強演講技巧。

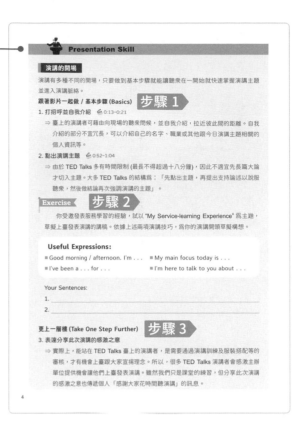

⑩ Your Talk

跟著書本上完每一堂課的演講技巧 (presentation skill) 後，搭配設計好的回饋表 (feedback sheet)，學生可分組或單獨上臺發表演講。其他同學可利用此份回饋表成為最佳的意見回饋者，將對於此演講的建議回饋給演講者。或是讓教師作為教學成果驗收之用。此回饋表附有裁切線，方便教師及同學撕下來，可以自行運用或分組使用，抑或是作為教師為學生評分演講表現之用途。背面為筆記頁 (NOTE)，可自由書寫，作為延伸筆記之用途。

⑪ Performance Evaluation Sheet

此份演講評估表 "Performance Evaluation Sheet"，共分成十個評分項目，每一個項目五個 level，每一個 level 兩分，總分共一百分。可依課程需求作為部分項目評估，也可用來當作整體評估，作為期末成果發表的評估表。同學跟著書本上完 10 堂課的演講技巧後，可選擇某一個課文主題，或是另擇主題，對全班演示完整的演講。其他同學可利用此表為演講者評分，或是讓教師作為教學成果驗收之用。

⑫ 附錄 —

▶ 演講技巧清單

彙整全書每一課的演講技巧，讓讀者一目瞭然。

⑬ 解析本 —

解析本提供參考解答和課文中譯。

目次 Contents

All pictures in this publication are authorized for use by: Depositphotos and Shutterstock.

演講影片清單

Unit	Topic	Speaker	QR code
1	"Am I Dying?" The Honest Answer	Matthew O'Reilly	
	Video https://www.ted.com/talks/matthew_o_reilly_am_i_dying_the_honest_answer		
2	A Precise, ThreeWord Address for Every Place on Earth	Chris Sheldrick	
	Video https://www.ted.com/talks/chris_sheldrick_a_precise_three_word_address_for_every_place_on_earth		
3	What I've Learned from My Autistic Brothers	Faith Jegede Cole	
	Video https://www.ted.com/talks/faith_jegede_what_i_ve_learned_from_my_autistic_brothers		
4	The 4 Ways Sound Affects Us	Julian Treasure	
	Video https://www.ted.com/talks/julian_treasure_the_4_ways_sound_affects_us		
5	Tough Truths About Plastic Pollution	Dianna Cohen	
	Video https://www.ted.com/talks/dianna_cohen_tough_truths_about_plastic_pollution		
6	A Bath Without Water	Ludwick Marishane	
	Video https://www.ted.com/talks/ludwick_marishane_a_bath_without_water		
7	Why You Should Care About Whale Poo	Asha de Vos	
	Video https://www.ted.com/talks/asha_de_vos_why_you_should_care_about_whale_poo		
8	The Danger of Silence	Clint Smith	
	Video https://www.ted.com/talks/clint_smith_the_danger_of_silence		
9	Want to Be an Activist? Start with Your Toys	McKenna Pope	
	Video https://www.ted.com/talks/mckenna_pope_want_to_be_an_activist_start_with_your_toys		
10	Lies, Damned Lies and Statistics (About TED Talks)	Sebastian Wernicke	
	Video https://www.ted.com/talks/lies_damned_lies_and_statistics_about_tedtalks		

Unit 01

Presentation Skill | Speech Opening and Closing

How Are We to Face Death?

Session 1

 Warm-up

Discuss the following questions with your classmates.

1. What does "death" mean to you? (可複選)

   (A) A pathway to paradise.

   (B) A journey to the next life.

   (C) A route leading to nothing.

   (D) A part of the natural life cycle.

   (E) A lesson to learn that life is important.

2. If you had only one day to live, what would you do in your last moments? (可複選)

   (A) Do nothing but wait.

   (B) Spend all your money.

   (C) Follow your normal routine.

   (D) Get together with your loved ones.

   (E) Write down your final words in a will.

Watch the Video

Scan the QR code on the left to play the video.

Speaker: Matthew O'Reilly

Topic: "Am I Dying?" The Honest Answer

 Track-01

In the distant future, medical science may give humankind the gift of immortality. For now, though, no one can avoid death. Many people prefer not to think about the fact that one day they will **perish**[1]. The idea fills them with **terror**[2], so they push it out of their mind. However, the way we think about our own death, **regardless of**[3] our religions, could help us lead a happy life and even find **comfort**[4] as it comes to an end.

Elizabeth Kübler-Ross spent her **career**[5] studying the psychology of people who have been told of their imminent death. She found that their **reaction**[6] usually follows a **pattern**[7]. First, they find themselves unable to grasp the painful truth so they deny it exists. Then, they **respond**[8] with anger, which in extreme cases can even lead to a violent **incident**[9]. In the next stage, the individual's mind becomes filled with sad remembrances and past **regrets**[10]. The final stage is **acceptance**[11] of death. People who are dying face a **dilemma**[12]: whether to continue the fight for life or to accept that their life will soon come to an end. After assessing their options, they usually accept the **critical**[13] situation that they are dying. Most people are able to find **forgiveness**[14] in their hearts in this final stage shortly prior to passing away.

While death comes to us all, we should never let our fear of death prevent us from living our life to the full. As the philosopher Immanuel Kant **observed**[15], "a person who is always worried about losing his life will never be able to enjoy it."

Vocabulary

 Track-02

◆ Words for Production

1. perish (v.) 死亡	2. terror (n.) 恐懼	3. regardless of (prep.) 不論
4. comfort (n.) 慰藉	5. career (n.) 職業	6. reaction (n.) 反應
7. pattern (n.) 模式	8. respond (v.) 回應	9. incident (n.) 事件
10. regret (n.) 遺憾	11. acceptance (n.) 接受	12. dilemma (n.) 兩難
13. critical (adj.) 關鍵性的	14. forgiveness (n.) 寬恕	15. observe (v.) 察覺；評述

◆ Words for Recognition

immortality (n.) 永生	grasp (v.) 理解	remembrance (n.) 回憶
assess (v.) 評估	prior to ... (prep.) 在…之前	

Session 2

Watch the Video Again

Exercise

1. Why wouldn't Matthew O'Reilly tell the dying the truth that they were going to die in the first place?

   _____

2. Write down the three patterns that Matthew O'Reilly has observed when he tells people the truth that they are dying.

   (1) _____

   (2) _____

   (3) _____

Presentation Skill

演講的開場

演講有多種不同的開場，只要做到基本步驟就能讓聽眾在一開始就快速掌握演講主題並進入演講脈絡。

跟著影片一起做 / 基本步驟 (Basics)

1. 打招呼並自我介紹 🎬 0:13-0:21

⇒ 臺上的演講者可藉由向現場的聽眾問候，並自我介紹，拉近彼此間的距離。自我介紹的部分不宜冗長，可以介紹自己的名字、職業或其他跟今日演講主題相關的個人資訊等。

2. 點出演講主題 🎬 0:52-1:04

⇒ 由於 TED Talks 多有時間限制 (最長不得超過十八分鐘)，因此不適宜先長篇大論才切入主題。大多 TED Talks 的結構為：「先點出主題，再提出支持論述以說服聽眾，然後做結論再次強調演講的主題」。

▷ Exercise

　　你受邀發表服務學習的經驗，試以 "My Service-learning Experience" 為主題，草擬上臺發表演講的講稿。依據上述兩項演講技巧，為你的演講開頭草擬構想。

Useful Expressions:

■ Good morning / afternoon. I'm . . .　■ My main focus today is . . .

■ I've been a . . . for . . .　■ I'm here to talk to you about . . .

Your Sentences:

1. _____

2. _____

更上一層樓 (Take One Step Further)

3. 表達分享此次演講的感激之意

⇒ 實際上，能站在 TED Talks 臺上的演講者，是需要通過演講訓練及服裝搭配等的審核，才有機會上臺跟大家宣揚理念。所以，很多 TED Talks 演講者會感激主辦單位提供機會讓他們上臺發表演講。雖然我們只是課堂的練習，但分享此次演講的感激之意也傳遞個人「感謝大家花時間聽演講」的訊息。

4. 說明激發此次演講的背後動機

⇒ 也許是教師指定的演講主題，也許是自己想談論的議題，但無論是哪一種，個人的思想和經歷有可能影響聽眾反思自己的行為，甚至改變人們對這個世界的看法。將這些主題發想的動機明確告訴聽眾，尤其以自己深刻經歷的故事最能感動人。

▶ Exercise

延續相同主題 "My Service-learning Experience"，依據上述兩項演講技巧，為你的演講開頭草擬構想。

Useful Expressions:

- I'm grateful for . . .
- I appreciate . . .
- I used to think that . . . but . . .

Your Sentences:

3. _____

4. _____

演講的結尾

結尾要呼應前面提到的重點，達成前後連貫的目的並為演講劃下完美句點。

跟著影片一起做 / 基本步驟 (Basics)

5. 講述小故事回應前面的要點 4:10–5:03

⇒ 演講者的時間有限，臺上的每分鐘都是關鍵。準備講稿時，並非想到什麼就說什麼。演練時，若發現與主題無關的想法或訊息，請務必刪除。換句話說，你所呈現的小故事或軼事必須要直接回應你想傳達的訊息。

6. 重複想要聽眾記住的重點，為演講做摘要 5:07–5:21

⇒ 有些人會在演講的結尾介紹新的想法，這麼做很容易讓聽眾忘記你原先想傳達的重點。演講收尾的重點應放在再次重申你想要傳遞的主題。參考演講的開頭是如何介紹今日主題，然後用不同的字詞再次表達相同的意念。

▶ Exercise

延續相同主題 "My Service-learning Experience"，依據上述兩項演講技巧，為你的演講結尾草擬構想。

Useful Expressions:

- I've come to realize . . .
- In conclusion . . .

Your Sentences:

5. _____

6. _____

更上一層樓 (Take One Step Further)

7. 給聽眾建議

⇒ 英文說 "Actions speak louder than words."。改變聽眾想法不夠，成功的演講者可激發他人行動力。試著給聽眾建議，鼓勵他們具體實踐並改變行為。

8. 為演講劃下句點

⇒ 演講有開頭，當然也有結尾。必須清楚告知聽眾演講到此結束，劃下句點。

9. 感謝聽眾並開放問答

⇒ 如果時間允許，開放大約三分鐘的時間讓聽眾發問，藉此可以澄清先前模糊的概念。回答問題仍以聚焦主題為重，不宜談論其他延伸議題。

Exercise

延續相同主題 "My Service-learning Experience"，依據上述三項演講技巧，為你的演講結尾草擬構想。

Useful Expressions:

- I would suggest that . . .
- That's all for my talk / speech / presentation.
- Thank you. We have a few more minutes, so I'd be happy to take some questions from you.

Your Sentences:

7. _____

8. _____

9. _____

Your Talk

完成之前的練習後，整合演講的開頭 "Speech Opening" 和結尾 "Speech Closing" 的內容，使演講具有連貫性。班級以五至七人爲一組，延續相同主題 "My Service-learning Experience"。可分組互相練習或每組派一名學生上臺演示，其他同學完成下方回饋表。

Feedback Sheet for Unit 1 — Speech Opening and Closing

檢視演講者的演講並據以勾選下表，給予評論，幫助其發表更精煉。

班級：＿＿＿＿＿　組別：＿＿＿＿＿　姓名：＿＿＿＿＿

Speech Opening

☐ 1. 打招呼並自我介紹。

☐ 2. 點出演講主題。

☐ 3. 表達分享此次演講的感激之意。

☐ 4. 說明激發此次演講的背後動機。

Speech Closing

☐ 5. 講述小故事回應前面的要點。

☐ 6. 重複想要聽眾記住的重點，為演講做摘要。

☐ 7. 給聽眾建議。

☐ 8. 為演講劃下句點。

☐ 9. 感謝聽眾並開放問答。

Comments

NOTE

Unit 02

Presentation Skill **Giving Examples**

An Innovative Way to Guide You

Session 1

 Warm-up

Discuss the following questions with your classmates.

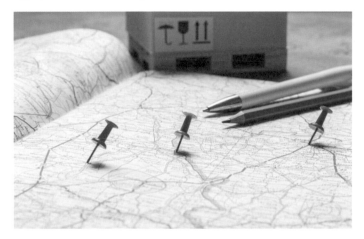

1. Have you had trouble writing an overseas address? What are some of the difficulties that you've encountered? Check 〔✓〕 the following boxes. (可複選)

   ☐ Complicated address spellings.

   ☐ Confusion about address lines.

   ☐ Uncertainty about correct translations.

   ☐ What information to put on the envelope.

2. What does "a three-word address for every place" mean to you?
   Check 〔✓〕 the following boxes. (可複選)

   ☐ It's only a slogan for a delivery company.

   ☐ It's no wonder that some mails get lost easily.

   ☐ It's much easier to locate a foreign place by three words.

   ☐ It can solve problems for those who live without an address.

Watch the Video

Scan the QR code on the left to play the video.

Speaker: Chris Sheldrick

Topic: A Precise, Three-Word Address for Every Place on Earth

READING

 Track-03

When Chris Sheldrick was working in the music business, he discovered a problem. Musicians and music **equipment** would often not arrive at a correct address. Working with a friend, he set out to redefine addresses by giving every spot on earth a **precise** address using just three words.

In a TED Talk, Chris Sheldrick explained that billions of people do not have addresses. There may be roads shown on a map with **vast** empty spaces beside them. However, **satellite** images show that these areas are filled with homes and businesses. These places hold a lot of **economic potential**, but the people **struggle** because they don't have addresses.

Sheldrick and his friend knew that GPS coordinates were too **complicated**, so they created three-meter **squares** for the entire surface of the earth instead. With 40,000 words available, they created three-word **combinations** to give each square a unique address. For example, an address could be "blocks. evenly.breed" or "famous.spice.writer." Each of these sets of three words acts as an identifier for a single square on the earth. Since it was **essential** for all people to be able to use the system, they created it in different languages as well.

Instead of **sticking with** the old address system, countries will find many useful **applications** when **adopting** three-word addresses. For example, signs using three-word addresses have been **distributed** in some places, allowing emergency services to navigate people in trouble. This system can also help to increase business efficiency and speed up the growth of infrastructure. In a word, three-word addresses help solve all these and many more problems.

Vocabulary

 Track-04

◆ **Words for Production**

1. equipment (n.) 器材	2. precise (adj.) 準確的	3. vast (adj.) 遼闊的
4. satellite (n.) 人造衛星	5. economic (adj.) 經濟的	6. potential (n.) 潛力
7. struggle (v.) 掙扎	8. complicated (adj.) 複雜的	9. square (n.) 正方形
10. combination (n.) 組合	11. essential (adj.) 極其重要的	12. stick with (phr.) 堅持
13. application (n.) 應用	14. adopt (v.) 採用	15. distribute (v.) 使分布

◆ **Words for Recognition**

coordinate (n.) 坐標	identifier (n.) 識別碼	navigate (v.) 導航
efficiency (n.) 效率	infrastructure (n.) 基礎建設	

Session 2

Watch the Video Again

Exercise

1. When the economist Hernando de Soto said "Without an address, you live outside the law. You might as well not exist," what did he imply?

   (A) One is safely protected by law if he / she has an address.

   (B) A person without an address is kept away from the whole world.

   (C) One can follow the law and live longer if he / she has an address.

   (D) The police won't be able to find a criminal if he doesn't have an address.

2. According to the video, which of the following might be a person's home address?

   (A) z.d.m   (B) zipper.jam.seven

   (C) akl.kbp.tlm   (D) medicine.t.q

3. Which of the following advantages can the three-word address system bring to the world? (複選題)

(A) The UN can deliver aid to the disaster areas.

(B) It only helps with the remote areas in some countries.

(C) People can find their destinations more easily in the wild.

(D) People can save money on the stamps when sending mails to friends.

 Presentation Skill

舉例

演講時，舉出實例可以使抽象的概念具體化，也可以讓聽眾理解並快速進入演講的主題情境。

跟著影片一起做 / 基本步驟 (Basics)

1. **舉出實例，引導聽眾的思路** 📽 1:07–1:46

⇒ 縱然有遠大的想法，但若沒有實際例子的驗證，會讓你的演講給人「紙上談兵」或流於空談的印象。在一篇演講當中，你可能會提出三個論述，其中至少要有兩個論述加入自身 (或他人) 實例、新聞資料或統計數字等，可使你的演講內容豐富又具有說服力。

2. **傳遞比較複雜或抽象的概念時，運用實例來具體化** 📽 2:40–3:05

⇒ 用說故事的方式來舉例是再好不過了，大家都愛聽故事。但如果要傳遞比較複雜或抽象的概念時，可以藉由具體的圖表 (chart)、照片、圖片、地圖或是示意圖 (diagram) 來輔助訊息的傳達。如下圖所示，藉由示意圖顯示牛隻的各部位牛肉。

Exercise

　　試以 "The Convenience of _____" 爲主題，草擬上臺發表演講的講稿。依據上述兩項演講技巧，說明一項科技產品 (如手機、照相機、電腦等) 所帶來的生活便利性 (convenience)。

2

Useful Expressions:

■ My . . . brings convenience to my life, like . . .

■ I do many things on . . . For example . . .

Topic: The Convenience of _____

Your Sentences:

1. _____

　 _____

2. _____

　 _____

更上一層樓 (Take One Step Further)

3. 用圖片舉例，解釋例子更容易

⇒ 我們常說「有圖有眞相」，因此，試著在簡報中加入圖片，讓聽衆有不同的視覺刺激，使例子更容易被理解。

4. 舉例搭配說明，能更有條理地解釋清楚

⇒ 示意圖指的是有圖片再加上文字說明。簡報中加入示意圖可以更清楚說明你想傳遞的訊息。

5. 重複強調重點，加深聽衆印象

⇒ 聽衆在接收過多資訊時，難以在短時間內消化並理解演講的內容。因此，你可以在結尾或是演講的過程中多強調重點，加深聽衆的印象。

延續相同主題 "The Convenience of _____",依據上述三項演講技巧,爲你的演講草擬構想。

Useful Expressions:

■ As you can see from this slide . . .

■ As a . . . my time is limited, so I . . .

■ . . . has / have certainly made my life much more convenient.

■ . . . has / have enabled me to do various tasks all at the same time.

Your Sentences:

3. _____

_____

4. _____

_____

5. _____

_____

Schedule Management

> **補充說明** 上方示意圖是用來說明手機可協助整理資料及其帶來的生活便利性。你可以遵循上述方式,尋找適當的示意圖,放在簡報中。

Your Talk

　　完成之前的練習後，嘗試加入本課所提到的各種舉例技巧，適度地增修字句，使演講更爲完整。班級以五至七人爲一組，延續相同主題 "The Convenience of ＿＿＿＿＿"。可分組互相練習或每組派一名學生上臺演示，其他同學完成下方回饋表。

Feedback Sheet for Unit 2 — Giving Examples
檢視演講者的演講並據以勾選下表，給予評論，幫助其發表更精煉。
班級：＿＿＿＿＿　組別：＿＿＿＿＿　姓名：＿＿＿＿＿

Giving Examples

☐ 1. 舉出實例，引導聽眾的思路。
☐ 2. 傳遞比較複雜或抽象的概念時，運用實例來具體化。
☐ 3. 用圖片舉例，解釋例子更容易。
☐ 4. 舉例搭配說明，能更有條理地解釋清楚。
☐ 5. 重複強調重點，加深聽眾印象。

Comments

NOTE

Unit 03

Autistic People Are Different and That's OK

Session 1

 Warm-up

Discuss the following question with your classmates.

How much do you know about autism (自閉症)?

Check 〔✓〕 the following boxes. (可複選)

☐ There is no known cause of or cure for autism.

☐ People with autism get upset by small changes in the surroundings.

☐ Autistic people tend to avoid eye contact and prefer to be alone.

☐ Autism's most obvious signs may appear between 2 and 3 years of age.

☐ People with autism have difficulty understanding other people's feelings.

☐ Early intervention programs for young children with autism are effective in improving IQ, language ability, and social interaction.

Watch the Video

Scan the QR code on the left to play the video.

Speaker: Faith Jegede Cole

Topic: What I've Learned from My Autistic Brothers

 Track-05

The number of people **diagnosed**[1] with autism is increasing worldwide. Autistic people think in ways that bypass the "**normal**"[2] ways of understanding the world around them, which is why some autistic people lack social skills. However, this also gives some autistic people a special **gift**[3], such as an **extraordinary**[4] memory. In various cases, some autistic people with **incredible**[5] musical or mathematical talents will leave you **speechless**[6]! In recent years, autism researchers have launched campaigns to raise awareness of this common **disorder**[7].

On April 2ⁿᵈ every year, World Autism Awareness Day is celebrated around the world. One of the main goals is to highlight the **frustrations**[8] autistic people face. It also seeks to reduce the **prejudice**[9] shown toward people with autism. By promoting people's understanding of autism, it is hoped that there will be greater acceptance of these **innocent**[10] people.

Autistic people often find it hard to "fit in," as they are not considered normal and their individuality is seen as weird. As members of a caring society, we should not **overlook**[11] the needs of autistic people, and in fact, we ought to find ways to help them fulfill their potential.

With rates of autism on the rise, it is **obvious**[12] that we all have a role to play in the **pursuit**[13] of this challenging goal. No matter what your political, cultural, or **religious**[14] background is, find out how you can make a difference on World Autism Awareness Day. It might be difficult for us to accept them unconditionally, but we could at least try to make some **sacrifices**[15] to include them in our society.

Vocabulary

 Track-05

◆ Words for Production

1. diagnose (v.) 診斷	2. normal (adj.) 正常的	3. gift (n.) 天賦，才能
4. extraordinary (adj.) 非凡的	5. incredible (adj.) 不可思議的	6. speechless (adj.) 說不出話的，啞口無言的
7. disorder (n.) 病症	8. frustration (n.) 挫折	9. prejudice (n.) 偏見
10. innocent (adj.) 無辜的；天真無邪的	11. overlook (v.) 忽視	12. obvious (adj.) 明顯的
13. pursuit (n.) 追求，追尋	14. religious (adj.) 宗教的	15. sacrifice (n.) 犧牲

◆ Words for Recognition

autistic (adj.) 自閉症的	bypass (v.) 避開；忽視	individuality (n.) 特質，個性
challenging (adj.) 具挑戰性的	unconditionally (adv.) 無條件地	

Session 2

Watch the Video Again

Exercise

1. According to the video, which of the following is **NOT** the characteristic that Faith's autistic brothers have?

   (A) Never telling a lie.

   (B) Sharing love unconditionally.

   (C) Seeing the world with prejudice.

   (D) Having a pure and innocent nature.

2. Which of the following is the main idea that the speaker wants to convey to the audience?

(A) To introduce high-functioning autism.

(B) To provide solutions for children with autism.

(C) To promote language development in children with autism.

(D) To inform audience that people with autism can be extraordinary.

3. What ideas or thoughts would you like to share with your classmates after watching the video? Write down your ideas or thoughts.

_____

_____

 Presentation Skill

説故事

大多數人喜歡聽故事，你會發現當演講者在分享故事時，聽眾的專注力最高。利用以下的技巧可以幫助你把故事說得動聽而有趣。

跟著影片一起做 / 基本步驟 (Basics)

1. **提出要求或問題，先跟聽眾互動**　0:10-0:15

⇒ 你的要求或提問必須跟你要分享的故事有關，就像是鋪梗，為了要一把抓住聽眾的專注力。

2. **介紹故事的主要人物，架構故事脈絡**　0:15-1:35

⇒ 說明故事主角與自身的關係，並介紹主角的個性特質和相關細節，讓聽眾逐漸進入故事脈絡。

3. **陳述故事想傳遞的核心價值，為演講做結尾**　4:20-5:07

⇒ 每個故事都有想傳遞的核心價值，述說完故事，要記得清楚陳述故事帶來的啟發，為演講劃下句點。

Exercise

青少年的次文化，如角色扮演 (cosplay)、電子競技 (esports)、社團成果發表 (year-end performance)、粉絲 (fan) 追星等，常不爲大人所理解因而產生偏見 (prejudice)。試以 "What I've Learned from _____" 爲主題，草擬上臺發表演講的講稿，依據上述三項演講技巧，利用說故事的方式，澄清人們對某事物或某觀念的誤解。

3

Useful Expressions:

■ Today I have just one request.

■ I'd like to introduce you to . . .

■ I recall . . . , and I realize that . . .

Topic: What I've Learned from _____

Your Sentences:

1. _____

2. _____

3. _____

更上一層樓 (Take One Step Further)

4. 引導聽眾深入探索主題特質

⇒ 爲突顯主角特質或強調主題特色，可以引導聽眾深入探索主角或主題的特質，或從不同的角度切入，提供更寬廣的視野，避免描述過於空泛。

5. 專注於故事本身，刪除不必要的細節

⇒ 注意聽眾的反應，如果發現聽眾開始分心或不耐煩，就要盡快陳述細節或做適當刪減，帶領聽眾進入故事重點。

6. 撰寫提示手卡，依序串聯細節使故事流暢

⇒ 按照時間順序，將故事重點的關鍵字抄寫在手卡上，避免遺漏細節。陳述細節及心得時，首重將自身的經歷和體會分享給聽眾，增加演講的豐富性及趣味性。

延續相同主題 "What I've Learned from _____",依據上述三項演講技巧,
爲你的演講草擬構想。

Useful Expressions:

■ If you take a closer look at . . . , you'll appreciate . . .

■ He / She . . . in a way that most people cannot.

■ Facing criticism / difficulty . . .

Your Sentences:

4. (1) _____

   (2) _____

   (3) _____

6. 提示手卡：

開頭 → 1

主角名字：_____

主角跟你的關係：_____

_____

主角的個性特質：_____

與主題相關的重要事件一：

_____

_____

_____

_____

2

與主題相關的重要事件二：

_____

_____

故事衝突點／問題：_____

_____

_____

_____

_____

你的省思：_____

_____

_____

你的省思：_____

_____

_____

→ 3 → 結尾

Your Talk

完成之前的練習後，嘗試加入本課所提到的各種說故事技巧，適度地增修字句，使演講更爲完整。班級以五至七人爲一組，延續相同主題 "What I've Learned from _____"。可分組互相練習或每組派一名學生上臺演示，其他同學完成下方回饋表。

Feedback Sheet for Unit 3 — Telling Stories

檢視演講者的演講並據以勾選下表，給予評論，幫助其發表更精煉。

班級：_____ 組別：_____ 姓名：_____

Telling Stories

☐ 1. 提出要求或問題，先跟聽眾互動。

☐ 2. 介紹故事的主要人物，架構故事脈絡。

☐ 3. 陳述故事想傳遞的核心價值，為演講做結尾。

☐ 4. 引導聽眾深入探索主題特質。

☐ 5. 專注於故事本身，刪除不必要的細節。

☐ 6. 撰寫提示手卡，依序串聯細節使故事流暢。

Comments

NOTE

Session 1

 Warm-up

Compare the following two pictures and discuss the following question with your classmates.

Before   **After**

What do you think is the possible cause(s) of keeping your audience focused? Check 〔✓〕 the possible cause(s) below, and explain your reason(s) to the class.

☐ Reading from the slides.   ☐ Using graphics.

☐ Cutting unnecessary texts.   ☐ Having no eye contact.

☐ Interacting with the audience.   ☐ Giving a long presentation.

☐ Relating your information to your audience. ☐ Using sounds.

☐ Other(s): _____

Watch the Video

Scan the QR code on the left to play the video.

Speaker: Julian Treasure

Topic: The 4 Ways Sound Affects Us

READING

 Track-07

We live in an environment bathed in sound, and in this constantly changing soundscape we depend on ears to help us in everyday life. It is therefore hard to imagine what life would be like without sound.

For most people, it would be **dreadful**[1] to live without sound. What's more, the sounds we hear give us **valuable**[2] information, from the beep of our microwave to **recognizing**[3] someone's voice.

Sound is obviously **associated**[4] with communication and signaling. However, it plays an important role in our lives in other ways too. Just think how music can **transform**[5] one's **emotions**[6], for example. Music enters our **consciousness**[7], helping the mind to release any **suppressed**[8] negative feelings. Sound can also result in behavioral changes, including **inappropriate**[9] ones. Studies have shown it is harder to do cognitive tasks in a noisy office. Noise clearly **affects**[10] worker **productivity**[11], and it can have a huge **impact**[12] on quality of life as well. Living next to noisy neighbors can certainly affect your psychological well-being. Fortunately, listening to sounds corresponding to your desired mood can be helpful. For instance, peaceful sounds like waves on a beach can be incredibly **soothing**[13] and can even help protect against the **damaging**[14] effects of stress. It's **reassuring**[15] to know that certain sounds can also have a positive physiological effect, such as reducing blood pressure.

Let's give our sense of hearing a round of applause. You only get one pair of ears so take good care of them. Hopefully, they will last well into your golden years!

Vocabulary

 Track-08

◆ Words for Production

1. dreadful (adj.) 可怕的	2. valuable (adj.) 有用的	3. recognize (v.) 辨認
4. associate (v.) 連結	5. transform (v.) 大幅改變	6. emotion (n.) 情緒
7. consciousness (n.) 意識	8. suppress (v.) 壓抑	9. inappropriate (adj.) 不恰當的
10. affect (v.) 影響	11. productivity (n.) 生產效率	12. impact (n.) 影響
13. soothing (adj.) 使人平靜的，可慰藉的	14. damaging (adj.) 有害的	15. reassuring (adj.) 令人感到寬慰的

◆ Words for Recognition

soundscape (n.) 音景	behavioral (adj.) 行為的	cognitive (adj.) 認知的
psychological (adj.) 心理的	physiological (adj.) 生理的	

Session 2

Watch the Video Again

Exercise

1. What is this TED Talk mainly about?

   (A) To introduce four golden rules for commercial sound.

   (B) To explain how inappropriate sound harms our health.

   (C) To provide information of advanced sound technology.

   (D) To transform our relationship with the sounds around us.

2. According to this TED Talk, which of the following is the most appropriate sound when you need to finish a report in time?

   (A) Office noise.   (B) Techno music.

   (C) Birdsong.   (D) Alarm clock rings.

3. The following are different types of outcomes in the way sound affects us. Fill in the blanks with the correct item (A–D).

(A) Cognitive.　　　(B) Psychological.　　(C) Behavioral.　　(D) Physiological.

(1) _____	(2) _____
◆ A fight-or-flight response ◆ Affecting breathing and heart rate	◆ Affecting our emotions ◆ Finding birdsong reassuring
(3) _____	(4) _____
◆ Affecting productivity in offices ◆ Not understanding two people talking at once	◆ Affecting sales for retailers ◆ Moving away from unpleasant sounds to pleasant sounds

 Presentation Skill

利用圖片、圖表、音效爲演講加分

　　大家都會使用 PowerPoint 軟體,但要製作出一份精美的簡報檔案需要一些技巧。好的簡報架構、適當的影音效果或精簡的內文等技巧,可以爲你的簡報與口語表達加分不少。

跟著影片一起做 / 基本步驟 (Basics)

1. 利用圖片傳遞資訊 🎬 0:23–0:27

⇒ 英文有句話說 "A picture is worth a thousand words." (一張圖勝過千言萬語)。簡報呈現的不是你的逐字講稿,而是聽衆看圖片就能理解的觀念。所以簡報畫面盡可能以圖片呈現,才能傳遞強而有力的訊息並加深聽衆印象。

2. 運用音效加深聽衆印象 🎬 0:56–1:14 & 2:43–2:53

⇒ 適當的聲音效果可以引發聽衆的情感並觸發他們的情緒。如同這篇演講呈現的音效,如果演講者只是口述愉悅的海浪聲音,或讓聽衆自行想像討人厭的鑽孔機聲音,其傳遞的訊息會薄弱許多。相較於此,演講者直接加入音效,讓聽衆實際透過聽覺直接感受聲音帶來的愉悅或煩躁。

Exercise

　　兒時回憶總是充滿酸甜苦辣,現在回憶起來,多半是溫馨美好的記憶。試以 "My Best Childhood Memory" 爲題,草擬上臺發表演講的講稿。依據上述所提之演講及簡報製作技巧,提供一張兒時的照片,分享你美好的兒時記憶。步驟如下:

1. 選擇一張兒時記憶的照片放在簡報中，並試著介紹這張照片。

2. 選擇兒時記憶事件中，令你印象深刻的聲音，放入簡報並試著總結。

Useful Expressions:

- This is a picture of me taken when . . .
- We used to . . . listening to / watching / seeing / enjoying / eating . . .
- That was really my best childhood memory.

Your Sentences:

1. _____

_____

2. _____

_____

_____

_____

更上一層樓 (Take One Step Further)

3. 加入圖表，簡化資訊，數字明列在投影片上 　🎬 2:10, 3:20, 4:15

⇒ 把複雜的文字資訊簡化成圖表，可以協助聽眾快速汲取你提供的訊息，尤其在比較兩者之間的差異或呈現時間順序的變化時，柱狀圖 (bar graph)、折線圖 (line graph)、圓餅圖 (pie chart)、流程圖 (flow chart) 等都是有效傳達資訊的圖表。此外，與其念複雜的數字，不如將數字明列在投影片上，既可突顯數字量化上的差異，也可方便聽眾看清楚並快速理解數字含意。對英文不是母語的人來說，大多數人無法快速理解透過口語傳達的數字。此外，各國表達數字的方式也不盡相同 (例如：中文說「十萬」，英文說 "one hundred thousand")，因此演講內容若有提到數字，最好列在投影片上。

柱狀圖	折線圖	圓餅圖	流程圖

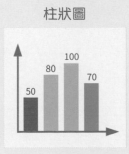
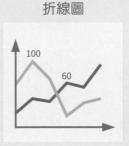

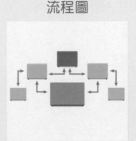

4. 分三步驟介紹圖表

⇒ 演講者可分三步驟介紹圖表所傳遞的訊息：(1) 簡介圖表類型。(2) 說明圖表資訊。

(3) 強調圖表重點。

(可參考下方 Useful Expressions 完成介紹圖表的三步驟)

5. 簡化文字內容

⇒ 投影片最好以列點方式 (bullet points) 來呈現要表達的重點，簡報上的文字越簡潔越好，避免艱澀的名詞或複雜的句型結構。以英文簡報為例，一張投影片建議不要超過五行字，一行不要超過五個字。

Exercise

下面兩個圓餅圖，分別呈現 1990 年和 2018 年青少年時間分配的調查結果。試依據上述演講及簡報製作技巧，比較這兩個圖表，為你的演講草擬構想。

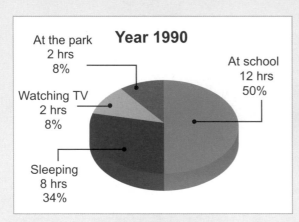
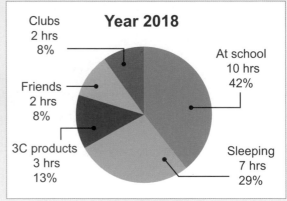

Useful Expressions:

3 Steps to Describe a Chart:

(1) This . . . chart / graph shows / describes . . .

(2) These colors / lines / dots / figures show . . .

(3) The key point is that . . . / Please note that . . .

Your Sentences:

4. (1) _____

(2) _____

(3) _____

Your Talk

完成之前的練習後，嘗試加入本課所提到的各種影音補充技巧，如利用圖片傳遞訊息，並適度地增修字句，使演講更爲完整。班級以五至七人爲一組，延續相同主題 "My Best Childhood Memory"。可分組互相練習或每組派一名學生上臺演示，其他同學完成下方回饋表。

> **Feedback Sheet for Unit 4 — Using Effective Visuals and Sounds**
> 檢視演講者的演講並據以勾選下表，給予評論，幫助其發表更精煉。
> 班級：＿＿＿＿＿　組別：＿＿＿＿＿　姓名：＿＿＿＿＿

Using Effective Visuals and Sounds

☐ 1. 利用圖片傳遞資訊。

☐ 2. 運用音效加深聽眾印象。

☐ 3. 加入圖表，簡化資訊，數字明列在投影片上。

☐ 4. 分三步驟介紹圖表。

☐ 5. 簡化文字內容。

Comments

NOTE

Presentation Skill   **Adding Twists**

A Long-Term Solution to Plastic Pollution

Session   1

 ### Warm-up

Look at the two pictures below and think about what you would say about each picture. Write down your opinions in the following blanks and share them with your classmates.

Picture 1: _____

_____

_____

_____

Picture 2: _____

_____

_____

_____

Watch the Video

Scan the QR code on the left to play the video.

Speaker: Dianna Cohen

Topic: Tough Truths About Plastic Pollution

READING

 Track-09

¹**Plastic** pollution is something everyone should be ²**concerned** about. The ³**primary** issue is our love of plastic bottles. One million plastic bottles are bought globally every minute. Only 7% gets recycled and the rest is buried or incinerated, or ends up in the ocean.

Once in the ocean, all that ⁴**disposable** plastic becomes trapped in gyres, which are circular ocean currents, resulting in enormous patches of plastic garbage. Slowly, tiny pieces chip off the plastic. ⁵**Marine** life eats these bits of plastic, and the ⁶**toxins** they contain eventually enter the human food chain.

But what are the ⁷**alternatives** to plastic? The simplest way to avoid using plastic is to use a bottle or ⁸**container** made of another material. Glass and stainless steel are the most obvious choices. In addition, a number of initiatives and ⁹**proposals** have been put forward to deal with the plastic pollution crisis. The Plastic Pollution Coalition believes that the three "Rs" of reducing, reusing, and recycling are not enough. It ¹⁰**aims** to raise awareness of a fourth "R": ¹¹**refuse**. If we refuse to buy products ¹²**packaged** in plastic, this will ¹³**generate** a demand for more ¹⁴**sustainable** packaging.

Plastic pollution is a serious threat to the health of our entire planet. Technology can certainly play a role in ridding our oceans of plastic. However, if our ¹⁵**intention** is to find a long-term solution, there is no more powerful a tool than consumer choice. Make your voice heard by saying "No" to plastic.

Vocabulary

 Track-10

◆ **Words for Production**

1. plastic (n.) 塑膠	2. concerned (adj.) 關切的；擔心的	3. primary (adj.) 主要的
4. disposable (adj.) 用過即丟的	5. marine (adj.) 海洋的	6. toxin (n.) 毒素
7. alternative (n.) 替代方案	8. container (n.) 容器	9. proposal (n.) 建議
10. aim (v.) 致力，旨在	11. refuse (v.) 拒絕	12. package (v.) 包裝
13. generate (v.) 產生，創造	14. sustainable (adj.) 對環境無害的	15. intention (n.) 打算，意圖

◆ **Words for Recognition**

incinerate (v.) 焚燒	gyre (n.) 海洋環流	chip (v.) 使碎裂
initiative (n.) 新措施	coalition (n.) 聯盟	

Session 2

Watch the Video Again

Exercise

Choose the words from the box below and fill in the following blanks.

(A) containers (B) awareness (C) packaged (D) recycle
(E) alternatives (F) refuse (G) bin (H) disposable

What You Can Do and Cannot Do to Help Reduce Plastic Pollution

Do's	Don'ts
1. Pick up the plastic and _____ it. 2. Teach people to choose _____. 3. Raise people's _____ of plastic pollution. 4. _____ single-use and disposable plastic.	1. Use _____ forks and knives. 2. Use plastic _____ to store food. 3. Buy plastic-_____ food in the supermarket. 4. Use plastic once and throw it in the _____.

 Presentation Skill

加入轉折

　　演講加入故事轉折 (twist)，可以給聽衆驚喜並爲演講增加精釆的內容。演講如果只有平鋪直敍，會讓聽衆容易猜到結局，反而失去耐心聽到最後。利用以下的技巧可以幫助你的演講更具戲劇性效果。

跟著影片一起做 / 基本步驟 (Basics)

1. 演講者身分的轉折　0:11-0:18

　⇒ 影片中的演講者 Dianna Cohen 原本是藝術創作者，在了解塑膠汙染後，成爲塑膠汙染聯盟的發起人。而若以學生的身分，在了解要分享的主題後，可以用類似的概念來設定身分轉換 (如社團發起人、假日志工、活動籌辦人等)。

2. 觀念的轉折　3:17-3:40

　⇒ Dianna Cohen 原本以爲把塑膠製品丟到垃圾桶就沒事，但卻發現在美國，只有不到 7% 的塑膠垃圾被回收處理。你也可以在演講中安插一個轉折，說明你在鑽研特定主題後所產生的轉變或所獲得的啓發。

3. 方法的轉折，提出實際可行之改善方法　3:52-4:07

　⇒ Dianna Cohen 指出原本回收所強調的 3Rs (reduce, reuse, and recycle) 已不夠用，要再增加第四個 R (refuse)。演講內容可以指出固有做法的不足，並提出方法的轉折以提供新解。可以試著以條列的方式，提出改善環境的方法。不要太顧慮文法，也無須在意想法是否新穎或老套，重點在於運用這個議題活化大腦，啓發更多分享靈感。

Exercise

　　不論是空氣汙染 (air pollution)、塑膠汙染 (plastic pollution) 或是水汙染 (water pollution)，各式各樣的汙染使我們的居住環境受到傷害。我們雖然能力有限，但一定可以做一些事讓我們的環境更美好。試以 "How We Can Help to Protect the Environment as a Teenager" 為題，草擬上臺發表演講的講稿，依據上述三項演講技巧，加入不同的轉折類型，使你的演講更精采。

Useful Expressions:

■ I am a(n) . . . , and I'm also a(n) . . .

■ You don't think twice about it. What is the reality behind that?

Your Sentences:

1. _____

_____

2. _____

_____

3. Please list several ways of protecting the environment in the blank space below.

更上一層樓 (Take One Step Further)

4. 生活型態的轉折

⇒ 可以在演講中說明，因爲對某個議題有更進一步的了解，改變了演講者或故事主角的生活方式，重新檢視舊有習慣的事物，並加以改善。

5. 聽眾與演講者角色互換的轉折

⇒ 演講者站在臺上極力宣傳某項理念，期待臺下的聽眾也能身體力行。在演講後段可提供方法，讓臺下聽眾有參與感，使他們相信只要照著方法做，也可以一起貢獻心力而有一番作爲。

Exercise

延續相同主題"How We Can Help to Protect the Environment as a Teenager"，依據上述演講技巧，爲你的演講草擬構想。

Useful Expressions:

■ I used to . . . , but now I'd rather . . .

■ This is a problem that we've created, and we can solve it. Whenever possible, . . .

Your Sentences:

4. _____

5. _____

Your Talk

　　完成之前的練習後，嘗試加入本課所提到的各種轉折技巧，適度地增修字句，使演講更爲完整。班級以五至七人爲一組，延續相同主題 "How We Can Help to Protect the Environment as a Teenager"。可分組互相練習或每組派一名學生上臺演示，其他同學完成下方回饋表。

Feedback Sheet for Unit 5 — Adding Twists
檢視演講者的演講並據以勾選下表，給予評論，幫助其發表更精煉。

班級：＿＿＿＿＿　組別：＿＿＿＿＿　姓名：＿＿＿＿＿

Adding Twists

☐ 1. 演講者身分的轉折。

☐ 2. 觀念的轉折。

☐ 3. 方法的轉折，提出實際可行之改善方法。

☐ 4. 生活型態的轉折。

☐ 5. 聽眾與演講者角色互換的轉折。

Comments

NOTE

Unit 06

Presentation Skill | **Adding Humor Elements**

Taking a Bath Without Water

Session 1

Warm-up

Look at the two pictures below and think about the following questions. Work in pairs and share your answers with your partner.

1. How long can you endure not taking a shower?

2. What are some of the things you need for taking a shower?

3. Imagine taking a waterless shower. How does it work?

Watch the Video

Scan the QR code on the left to play the video.

Speaker: Ludwick Marishane

Topic: A Bath Without Water

READING

 Track-11

Many inventions come about because there is a need to solve a problem. The history of medical science is full of examples of this concept, such as the invention of medicines which fight **infections**[1]. Antibiotics, for instance, have saved millions of lives. Sometimes inventions end up helping people in more ways than the inventor ever imagined.

One hot day in 2007, a South African teenager named Ludwick Marishane was hanging out with a friend who said, "Why doesn't somebody invent something that you can just put on your skin and you don't have to bathe?" Ludwick thought it was an interesting idea. He then tried to come up with a **lotion**[2] that people could put on their skin as a **substitute**[3] for having a bath. Without any **resources**[4] except for his cellphone and the Internet, he did a lot of research and finally invented a **formula**[5] that really worked. He got a patent for his product that he called DryBath. His next **puzzle**[6] was how to promote it. The young entrepreneur knew there would be a **demand**[7] for his product among rich people who appreciate convenience. However, he realized it could also be useful in areas with poor sanitation. For people who don't have **access**[8] to clean water, DryBath could **literally**[9] be a life-saver. According to **statistics**[10], a disease called trachoma affects 350 million people in Africa and leaves millions of people on the verge of being **permanently**[11] blind. Simply maintaining **cleanliness**[12] of one's face can prevent this disease. What's more, each DryBath **sachet**[13] saves about 80 liters of water.

Since he first started selling DryBath, Ludwick's business has thrived. Today his company **supplies**[14] customers from all over the world, including **multinational**[15] clients like the United Nations.

Vocabulary

 Track-12

◆ Words for Production

1. infection (n.) 感染	2. lotion (n.) 乳液	3. substitute (n.) 替代品
4. resource (n.) 資源	5. formula (n.) 配方	6. puzzle (n.) 難題
7. demand (n.) 需求	8. access (n.) 取用…的機會	9. literally (adv.) 簡直就是，名副其實地
10. statistics (n.) 統計 (數字)	11. permanently (adv.) 永久地	12. cleanliness (n.) 清潔
13. sachet (n.) 一小袋，一小包	14. supply (v.) 供應，供給	15. multinational (adj.) 跨國的，多國的

◆ Words for Recognition

patent (n.) 專利權	entrepreneur (n.) 創業者；企業家	sanitation (n.) 衛生設備
on the verge of (phr.) 幾乎…，瀕於…	thrive (v.) 生意興隆，蓬勃發展	

Session 2

Watch the Video Again

Exercise

1. Which of the following best describes the theme of the talk?

   (A) Every cloud has a silver lining.

   (B) Slow and steady wins the race.

   (C) Birds of a feather flock together.

   (D) Necessity is the mother of invention.

2. Besides skipping a bath, which of the following is **NOT** a side benefit the bath-substituting lotion brings to people?

   (A) To save water.

   (B) To save time for school.

   (C) To write a 400-page business plan.

   (D) To avoid being infected with trachoma (砂眼).

3. Like Ludwick Marishane's lotion, there are other interesting inventions in our lives. Can you provide any examples of them? Share them with your classmates.

 Presentation Skill

加入幽默元素

　　增加幽默元素到你的演講中，不僅可以讓聽眾專注於演講，還能使他們對演講印象深刻。因此，在演講中適當地加入一些幽默元素，可以爲演講增添趣味。有些人認爲幽默是天生的，但事實上，幽默是一項可以涵養及發展的演講技巧，參考下方步驟，可以讓演講變得風趣幽默。

跟著影片一起做 / 基本步驟 (Basics)

1. 有趣的對話或軼事 🎬 0:26–0:50

⇒ 幽默元素最好的來源就是自己本身的經驗。原本日常生活中不經意的對話，重新詮釋爲一段看似胡鬧但有趣的對談，再轉換成演講的幽默元素。例如：本來是 Ludwick Marishane 和朋友去河邊玩水做日光浴的玩笑話，卻成爲日後發明的好點子。重新詮釋對話時，要注意故事敍述的流暢性、生動的表情 (如假裝沉思)、肢體動作的搭配，以及聲音的抑揚頓挫。

2. 誇張的言語 (exaggeration) 🎬 1:33–1:44

⇒ 「發明的產品，就算不是爲了自己 (不喜歡洗澡的理由)，至少可以用來拯救世界吧。」Ludwick Marishane 用誇張的言語來強化自己產品的發想，成功地博得聽眾爆笑的回應。試試看把一般人放在超凡的情境中 (如Ludwick Marishane 拯救全世界)，或是把超凡的人放在日常一般的情境中 (如愛因斯坦數學很爛，沒通過大學入學考試)，這兩種方式都是很好的誇張幽默元素。

3. 開自己玩笑 🎬 4:36–5:00

⇒ Ludwick Marishane 因自己的創新發明得到許多獎項，而他所不能理解的卻是——這一切的光環都得歸功於自己不想洗澡的原因。他藉由開自己玩笑，並顯露個性缺點，去連接整篇演講的主題，以此幽默元素爲演講劃下完美的句點。

Exercise

　　花點時間回憶一個發生在你 (或周遭朋友) 身上的有趣故事。試以 "An Interesting Story About _____" 爲題，草擬上臺發表演講的講稿，依據上述三項演講技巧，加入幽默元素，使你的演講更精采。

Useful Expressions:

- I was wondering if / why . . .
- I intended to . . . , but it turned out that . . .
- I was expecting . . .

Topic: An Interesting Story About _____

Your Sentences:

1. _____
   _____

2. _____
   _____

3. _____
   _____

更上一層樓 (Take One Step Further)

4. 增加幽默元素在適當的地方

⇒ 大部分人沒那麼幸運,天生就具有幽默感,但幽默是可以學習得來的。不管你的講稿是否有趣,先打草稿,把自己想表達的東西寫下來,之後再回頭看講稿,試著把幽默元素放在適當的地方。(這項技巧需反覆練習幾次並花些時間才能完成。)

5. 笑話或軼事要簡短並連接演講的主題

⇒ 敘述笑話或軼事的長度不應超過一分鐘,太冗長的幽默故事讓人無法專注,也讓人失去耐心。另外,人人喜歡聽笑話,但單純只為娛樂聽眾而講笑話,卻沒有與主題相關的元素,會讓聽眾不解笑話的重點在哪裡,更失去演講的最終目的 —— 傳達你的想法及觀點。

6. 神情愉悅並面帶微笑,不幽默也沒關係

⇒ 敘說笑話或軼事時,可以神情愉悅並面帶微笑,但千萬不要明示聽眾你要開始說笑話,所以記得刪除 "Let me tell you a funny story." 之類的句子。有趣與否由聽眾決定,就算聽眾沒反應,依然繼續演講,就好像你敘述的軼事被當成一件嚴肅的事件來看待。幽默畢竟只是輔助你達成演講目的之次要元素,不是第一優先考量的要素。

6

備註 可以加入演講中的幽默元素還包括雙關語 (puns)、文字遊戲 (wordplay) 等，但這些元素的運用需要對語言及文化有更深入的了解才能掌握精髓。建議多欣賞 Sir Ken Robinson ──TED 講堂被觀賞最多次的演講者 ── 的演講，一窺幽默元素的完整呈現。

Exercise

延續相同主題 "An Interesting Story About _____"，依據上述三項演講技巧，為你的演講草擬構想。

Useful Expressions:

- I couldn't believe that . . .
- What's the point of telling the story?
- Instead of . . . , he / she / I . . .

Your Sentences:

4. _____

   _____

5. _____

   _____

6. _____

   _____

Your Talk

　　完成之前的練習後，嘗試加入本課所提到的各種增加幽默的技巧，如誇張的言語或表情，並適度地增修字句，使演講更爲完整。班級以五至七人爲一組，延續相同主題 "An Interesting Story About _____"。可分組互相練習或每組派一名學生上臺演示，其他同學完成下方回饋表。

Feedback Sheet for Unit 6 — Adding Humor Elements
檢視演講者的演講並據以勾選下表，給予評論，幫助其發表更精煉。

班級：_____　組別：_____　姓名：_____

Adding Humor Elements

☐ 1. 有趣的對話或軼事。

☐ 2. 誇張的言語 (exaggeration)。

☐ 3. 開自己玩笑。

☐ 4. 增加幽默元素在適當的地方。

☐ 5. 笑話或軼事要簡短並連接演講的主題。

☐ 6. 神情愉悅並面帶微笑，不幽默也沒關係。

Comments

NOTE

Unit 07

I Love Whale Poo and So Should You

Session 1

 Warm-up

Look at the following pictures of whales. Make sentences by putting the given words in the right order. The first one has been done for you.

1. (that is / ever lived / The blue whale (藍鯨) / the largest / creature / has)

   The blue whale is the largest creature that has ever lived.

2. (a form of tourism / has become / whale watching / around the world / Recently,)

   _____

3. (are capable of / Humpbacks (座頭鯨) and blue whales / traveling / without / thousands of miles / feeding)

   _____

4. (they must / for a long time, / breathe air regularly / underwater / can remain / Although whales)

   _____

Watch the Video

Scan the QR code on the left to play the video.

Speaker: Asha de Vos

Topic: Why You Should Care About Whale Poo

Whales are the mysterious giants of the animal kingdom. Once feared as monsters, whales are now admired for their incredible size and grace. More importantly, recent research has found that whales are essential for the health of our oceans.

It is well known that the blue whale is the largest animal. However, it is less widely known that whales play several vital roles in **ecosystems**. Believe it or not, whale poo is important because it plays an instrumental part in the **carbon** cycle. Even when whales die, they contribute to the **stability** of ocean habitats. Whale carcasses provide "island" habitats for many **species**, and their tissues feed the marine food web with essential nutrients.

Whales have long been hunted for their bones, meat, and fat. In the modern age, whale hunters have **drastically** reduced the populations of many whale species. Whales also face **multiple** threats from human activity. Pollution is especially detrimental to whale populations, and whales can become entangled in huge fishing nets. Given how important these **endangered** animals are to the oceans and to the whole planet, several international campaigns have been launched to protect them. The International Whaling Commission (IWC) was established to promote the **conservation** of whales and prevent them from being hunted to **extinction**. The IWC **banned** whaling in 1986, but not all countries agreed to **halt** their activities. Also, whaling is still allowed for scientific research, and **aboriginal** cultures can still hunt migrating whales using traditional methods.

Whales deserve to be respected and protected. The **destruction** of whale populations by **commercial** whalers may provide some people with short-term profits. However, if whales become extinct, they can never be replaced. By taking care of these graceful marine **mammals**[15], we can help protect the world's oceans and in turn the entire planet.

Vocabulary

 Track-14

◆ Words for Production

1. ecosystem (n.) 生態系統	2. carbon (n.) 碳	3. stability (n.) 穩定
4. species (n.) 物種	5. drastically (adv.) 急劇地	6. multiple (adj.) 各種的
7. endangered (adj.) 瀕危的	8. conservation (n.) 保育	9. extinction (n.) 絕種
10. ban (v.) 禁止	11. halt (v.) 停止	12. aboriginal (adj.) 原住民的
13. destruction (n.) 破壞	14. commercial (adj.) 營利的	15. mammal (n.) 哺乳動物

◆ Words for Recognition

instrumental (adj.) 功能性的	carcass (n.) 動物屍體	nutrient (n.) 養分
detrimental (adj.) 有害的	entangled (adj.) 被纏住的	

Session 2

Watch the Video Again

Exercise

1. According to Asha de Vos, why is saving whales critical?

    (A) Whales are cute animals.

    (B) Whales are ecosystem engineers.

    (C) Whales are rare and excellent swimmers.

    (D) Whales are the largest mammals on earth.

2. What are some of the things that whale poo do to the resiliency (恢復力) of the oceans? (複選題)

    (A) To bring nutrients to the shallow parts of waters.

    (B) To show whales have a very good digestive system.

    (C) To transport fertilizers in migration from place to place.

    (D) To help distribute nutrients both horizontally and vertically.

7

3. What are some of the things that whales' rotting carcasses do to maintain the stability and health of our seas? (複選題)

(A) To alter the geographic distribution of these whale falls (鯨落).

(B) To transport carbon from the atmosphere to the deep oceans.

(C) To serve as temporary shelters for small marine animals to hide.

(D) To provide a feast to some 400 different species in the deep oceans.

 Presentation Skill

肢體語言

演講除聲音所表達出來的語言文字之外，肢體也在傳遞訊息。好的肢體語言可以協助傳遞自信及正向的訊息給聽眾，讓你的演講更有說服力。

跟著影片一起做 / 基本步驟 (Basics)

1. **選好位置站定，可做小範圍地走動** 🎬 0:12–0:20

⇒ 在還沒開始演講前，走上舞臺站定位置的那一刻，就是你給聽眾的第一印象。挺直站好，可以傳遞這樣的訊息給聽眾：「你很鎮靜、有自信並已為這場演講做好萬全的準備。」進行演講時，可以做小距離範圍的移動，或者在固定位置上試著朝左右兩邊轉身，跟所有的聽眾互動。

2. 跟聽眾進行眼神接觸 🎬 0:30–0:47

⇒ 眼神也是跟聽眾互動的重點。站定位置後，以大約三秒的時間環顧四周、對聽眾微笑，可以給人不疾不徐的好印象。影片當中可見演講者 Asha de Vos 不會只盯著某處的聽眾看，她持續不斷地用堅定而不閃躲的眼神與全部的聽眾做眼神互動。

3. 適當而不誇張的手勢 🎬 5:11–5:33

⇒ 手勢是一種有助於傳達重點的肢體語言，適當而不誇張的手勢可以協助活化演講並強調重點。一般來說，雙手可以交叉輕握放在前方腰部的位置 (如下圖)。有重點要強調時，可以參考並學習影片最後面的片段：演講者張開雙手，邀請所有聽眾一起拯救鯨魚，之後並指向自己，強調做這些事不是為了鯨魚，而是為了我們自己。

7

有些人認爲學生只要念書就好，不必關心社會上的大小事。然而，事實上，關心社會議題，可以幫助我們拓展視野。這些議題讓我們跟外在環境產生連結，與我們每個人的生活息息相關。試以 "Why Should We Care About _____?" 爲題，草擬上臺發表演講的講稿，依據上述三項演講技巧，說服聽衆一起來關心某個社會議題，如流浪動物 (stray animals)、無家可歸者 (the homeless)、他人 (others) 等議題。下圖呈現演講方式的多元面向。

Useful Expressions:

- We should care about . . . because . . .
- By taking care of them, we are showing . . .
- If we want to ensure . . . , we must learn to . . . to accomplish this goal.

Topic: Why Should We Care About _____?

Your Sentences:

1. _____

   _____

2. _____

   _____

3. _____

   _____

更上一層樓 (Take One Step Further)

4. 利用手勢來表達數字及各步驟的先後順序

⇒ 參考下方的圖片及用語，利用手勢來表示數字，或說明各步驟的先後順序。

"I have **three reasons**."

"The **first step** . . . , the **second step** . . . , and the **third step** . . ."

5. 利用手勢來強調重點

⇒ 參考下方的圖片及用語，利用手勢來強調演講的重點。

"This is **why we should** care about . . ."

"The key point is **here**."

6. 利用手勢來表達大小、形狀等

⇒ 參考下方的圖片及用語，利用手勢來表達事物的多寡、大小、形狀等。

"It only takes you **this little time**."

"It is shaped **like this**."

7

延續相同主題 "Why Should We Care About _____?"，依據上述三項演講技巧，配合演講內容運用適當的肢體語言，為你的演講草擬構想。

Useful Expressions:

- I have three reasons . . .
- The key point is . . .
- It only takes you this little time to . . .

Your Sentences:

4. _____

_____

5. _____

_____

6. _____

_____

Your Talk

完成之前的練習後，嘗試加入本課所提到的各種肢體語言的技巧，適度地增修字句，使演講更為完整。班級以五至七人為一組，延續相同主題 "Why Should We Care About _____?"。可分組互相練習或每組派一名學生上臺演示，其他同學完成下方回饋表。

Feedback Sheet for Unit 7 — Sending the Physical Message

檢視演講者的演講並據以勾選下表，給予評論，幫助其發表更精煉。

班級：_____ 組別：_____ 姓名：_____

Sending the Physical Message

☐ 1. 選好位置站定，可做小範圍地走動。

☐ 2. 跟聽眾進行眼神接觸。

☐ 3. 適當而不誇張的手勢。

☐ 4. 利用手勢來表達數字及各步驟的先後順序。

☐ 5. 利用手勢來強調重點。

☐ 6. 利用手勢來表達大小、形狀等。

Comments

✓ 演講者跟你眼神接觸 _____ 次。

✓ 演講者的手勢有哪些動作，記錄下來：

NOTE

Unit 08

Presentation Skill | **Voice Inflection**

Stand Up and Speak Up!

Session 1

Warm-up

Martin Niemöller (1892–1984), a German anti-Nazi pastor (牧師), was put in jail for his opposition to the Nazi state control of the churches. Read the pastor's famous quote and answer the questions below.

When the Nazis came for the communists (共產黨員),

I remained silent;

I was not a communist.

When they locked up the social democrats (社會民主黨員),

I remained silent;

I was not a social democrat.

When they came for the trade unionists (工會會員),

I did not speak out;

I was not a trade unionist.

When they came for the Jews (猶太人),

I remained silent;

I was not a Jew.

Auschwitz Concentration Camp
(位於波蘭奧斯威辛的納粹集中營)

When they came for me,

there was no one left to speak out.

Questions:

1. Who does the word "they" refer to?

2. What did Martin Niemöller want to do when he wrote the above passage?

Watch the Video

Scan the QR code on the left to play the video.

Speaker: Clint Smith

Topic: The Danger of Silence

Everyone has witnessed something bad happening to someone, such as a traffic accident or friends **indulging**¹ in nasty gossip behind a classmate's back. Have you ever **reflected**² on why most people choose not to do or say anything in such situations? There are no easy answers, but the good news is that we all have the power to act when the time comes. The **principle**³ of taking action and **speaking up**⁴ is especially important in today's world.

Modern society is facing many **challenges**⁵: hate speech, bullying, **violence**⁶, racial tensions, and privilege, to name just a few. These issues **manifest**⁷ in all kinds of ways, and can even result in war and **genocide**⁸. In everyday life, you may encounter uncomfortable situations you would rather not get involved. When someone is taking drugs, you decide ignorance is your safest choice. When you see someone in a store steal something, it's not your problem. But here's the thing: Your silence is now part of the problem.

Of course, speaking up can be tough. Naturally, you may fear the **consequences**⁹, i.e., people speaking **critically**¹⁰ of you, or laughing at you. But that fear leaves behind a residue that slowly eats away at your dignity. Try to put yourself in the victim's shoes. Wouldn't you want others to stand up for you? Of course you would! Far too many people face hate and **discrimination**¹¹ every day. If you could make a difference by speaking up, would you still prefer the **shame**¹² of remaining silent? Would you want that on your conscience?

It takes courage to speak up, but no one needs to face this **battle**¹³ alone. Imagine a society in which more people **consciously**¹⁴ speak up for others. Together, let's **explore**¹⁵ ways of making the world a fairer place by speaking up when it is the right thing to do.

Vocabulary

 Track-16

◆ **Words for Production**

1. indulge in (phr.) 沉溺於	2. reflect (v.) 認真思考	3. principle (n.) 原則
4. speak up (phr.) 發表意見	5. challenge (n.) 挑戰	6. violence (n.) 暴力
7. manifest (v.) 顯現	8. genocide (n.) 種族滅絕	9. consequence (n.) 後果
10. critically (adv.) 批判性地	11. discrimination (n.) 歧視	12. shame (n.) 羞愧
13. battle (n.) 戰役	14. consciously (adv.) 自覺地，有意識地	15. explore (v.) 探究；探索

◆ **Words for Recognition**

privilege (n.) 特權	ignorance (n.) 忽視	residue (n.) 殘渣
dignity (n.) 尊嚴	conscience (n.) 良知	

Session 2

Watch the Video Again

Exercise

1. What does Clint Smith mean by saying, "I bit my lip, because apparently we needed her money more than my students needed their dignity"?

   (A) He regretted that he didn't raise enough money.

   (B) He kept silent because he wanted to raise more money.

   (C) He chose to speak up in order to gain his students' dignity.

   (D) He needed money because his students needed their dignity.

2. Which of the following is **NOT** used as a metaphor (隱喻) for silence in Clint Smith's talk?

   (A) A lion.　　　　　　　　　　(B) Katrina.

   (C) Rwandan genocide.　　　　　(D) The residue of fear.

8

3. Is there anything that you've kept silent about for a long time? Take time to think about the question and write down your answer in the following box.

Example:

I've kept silent about the fact that <u>some of my classmates are indifferent to bullying in school</u>. I've decided to speak up and make a change for <u>a safe learning environment</u>.

Your answer:

 Presentation Skill

聲音的變化

　　Clint Smith 在演講中提到,他常教導學生透過詩歌 (poetry) 探索生活中的沉默。本篇演講最大的特色在於他巧妙運用英文字彙的聲韻,使他的演講聽起來彷彿是一場語文詩歌的饗宴。

　　多聽幾次他的演講,可以清楚感受到其中對語言文字熟練的掌握,及對聲音抑揚頓挫的適度拿捏。儘管一般人很難寫出如此文情並茂的演講稿,但我們仍可以欣賞的角度,試著從中學習一些利用文字及聲音的好例子。

跟著影片一起做 / 基本步驟 (Basics)

1. 利用文字對比,強調反差 🎬 0:19–0:27 & 2:40–2:52

　　⇒ 演講就是文字的聲音表達,這篇演講一開始提到馬丁‧路德‧金恩博士的話。金恩博士的演講常用對比的方式來強調反差,並讓演講聚焦。金恩博士說:"In the end, we will remember **not the words of our enemies, but the silence of our friends**."。利用 "words / silence", "enemies / friends" 的文字反差,並加重這四個字的發音,即可成功強調重點並聚焦。同樣地,Clint Smith 在面對捐款婦人的偏見時,闡述自己:"I bit my lip, because apparently **we needed her money** more than **my students needed their dignity**.", 強調 "her money / their dignity" 的文字反差並加重發音來聚焦沉默的軟弱。

2. 停頓，讓聽眾集中注意力　🎬 1:34–1:54

⇒ 演講者在臺上舌粲蓮花吐出一連串的文字，臺下的聽眾可能已經聽得失神，這時突然的停頓，在聽覺上彷彿暫時劃下休止符，讓聽眾重新抬頭，注意聆聽接下來要傳遞的訊息。例如：Clint Smith 提到他似乎習慣妥協而放棄了許多東西，像是放棄了汽水、麥當勞、薯條、法式接吻以及其他很多事情。接續一連串放棄的事物後，是聲音的暫停，然後，以較緩慢的聲音速度陳述："But one year, I gave up speaking."，Clint 在 "**But one year**" 的前後都暫停、等候，藉此集中聽眾注意力，強調「爲了妥協而放棄，選擇沉默」的可怕。演講者成功地用聲音的速度，交織快慢和暫停，來突顯重點。

3. 利用句型重複強調重點　🎬 3:00–3:23

⇒ Clint Smith 爲了強調沉默 (silence) 所帶來的傷害，用重複的句型來反覆說明。例如："Silence is Rwandan genocide. Silence is Katrina. It is . . . It is . . ."，同樣的主詞反覆成爲句子開頭，聲音帶來的重複效果會讓聽眾專注並對演講者一再重複的字詞沉澱以及反思。

Exercise

　　思考一下，生活周遭有哪些人、事、物是你無法忍受，卻又一直保持沉默的？ (例如：cheating on exams、bullying、sexual or racial prejudice等) 你將上臺發表演講，試以 "The Danger of _____" 爲主題，依據上述三項演講技巧，藉由你的發聲以喚醒公民意識或修正偏見。

Useful Expressions:

■ In the end, we will remember not . . . but . . .

■ (pause) What if (pause) . . .

■ Bullying is . . . Bullying is . . . It is . . . It is . . .

Topic: The Danger of _____

Your Sentences:

1. _____

2. _____

3. _____

8

更上一層樓 (Take One Step Further)

4. 加重 (stress) 字詞的讀音做聲音變化

⇒ 句子裡加重音的字通常是有文字意義的內容字 (content words)，演講者會加重音來說某個字或數個字表示強調，而其他的字，則壓低音調。這樣一來有重音與無重音的字之間會產生明顯的差異性，聽眾可依據所聽到的重音變化，來理解演講者想強調的重點。例如："In the end, we will remember **NOT** the **WOUND** of **THOSE WHO ARE BULLIED**, **BUT** the **VIOLENCE** of **THOSE WHO BULLY**."，試著把強調的字加重讀音，會有強調的效果。

5. 拉長 (stretch) 字詞的讀音做聲音變化

⇒ 拉長字詞讀音也是一個用來做聲音變化藉以強調重點的好方法。拉長字詞讀音也為說話速度做了不同變化，可增加聽眾聽演講的興趣。可以拉長讀音的字詞可能是副詞或是形容詞，例如："No, this **CANNOT** be continued."。

6. 連音 (linking) 增加說話流暢性

⇒ 第一種連音指的是「子音連母音」：當一個字以子音結尾，而下一個字以母音開頭時，可以用連音的方式增加說話的流暢度，例如：當我們說 "Los Angeles" 會念 "Lo**s A**ngeles"，"Thank you" 會念 "Than**k y**ou"。另一種連音是「子音連子音」：當一個字的字尾和下一個字的字首發音相同或相似的子音 (如 [t]、[d] 或 [s]) 時，同一個音只要發一次，或是微頓後直接念出後面的音，例如："gas station" 會念 "ga**st**ation"，"sit down" 會念 "si**do**wn"。

Exercise

延續相同主題 "The Danger of _____"，依據上述三項演講技巧，配合演講內容展現聲音的變化及流暢性。

Useful Expressions:

■ Kids who bully / cheat / experience sexual prejudice are more likely to . . .

■ Every situation is different. In some cases . . .

■ Bullying / Cheating / Sexual prejudice is linked to . . .

Your Sentences:

4. _____

5. _____

6. _____

Your Talk

完成之前的練習後，嘗試加入本課所提到的各種聲音變化的技巧，適度地增修字句，使之前寫好的練習句子更具說服力。班級以五至七人爲一組，延續相同主題 "The Danger of _____"。可分組互相練習或每組派一名學生上臺演示，其他同學完成下方回饋表。

Feedback Sheet for Unit 8 — Voice Inflection

檢視演講者的演講並據以勾選下表，給予評論，幫助其發表更精煉。

班級：_____ 組別：_____ 姓名：_____

Voice Inflection

☐ 1. 利用文字對比，強調反差。

☐ 2. 停頓，讓聽眾集中注意力。

☐ 3. 利用句型重複強調重點。

☐ 4. 加重 (stress) 字詞的讀音做聲音變化。

☐ 5. 拉長 (stretch) 字詞的讀音做聲音變化。

☐ 6. 連音 (linking) 增加說話流暢性。

Comments

✓ 演講者停頓處想強調：

_____

_____

✓ 演講者加重的字詞有：

_____

_____

✓ 演講者拉長音的字詞有：

_____

_____

NOTE

Unit 09

Women ≠ Men

 ## Warm-up

Look at the two pictures below. Discuss the following questions with your classmates.

1. Who does household chores in your family?

2. Do you do any household chores? Why or why not?

3. From household chores to the workplace, gender equality (性別平等) is what many people strive for. In your opinion, which of the following is an appropriate description for gender equality? (可複選)

   (A) Males and females are the same on all preferences and abilities.

   (B) We must have equal numbers of gender representation in every field.

   (C) Judge a person based on their values, and not view them as good or bad purely based on their gender.

   (D) It is reasonable for males and females to have different legal rights in some cases, such as maternity leave (產假).

Watch the Video

Scan the QR code on the left to play the video.

Speaker: McKenna Pope

Topic: Want to Be an Activist? Start with Your Toys

READING

 Track-17

For over a hundred years, women's rights **activists**[1] have fought for equality. Their efforts were the **spark**[2] that started the women's movement. However, there is still much work to be done to achieve true **gender**[3] equality.

In the past, women **were supposed to**[4] stay at home. Although some women worked in commercial companies, most did traditionally "female" jobs like secretaries and maids. What's more, they were **discouraged**[5] from doing "male" jobs such as doctors and pilots. In the 1970s, women could finally have both a family and a career, which gave them an outlet for creativity. Today, women face fewer **obstacles**[6]. Nonetheless, even in Finland, which has policies **specifically**[7] for gender equality, most nurses are women and most engineers are men. Perhaps men and women just choose different jobs because of biological **features**[8] of the male and female brain. But the way men and women **market**[9] themselves probably also plays a role. In the end though, does it **matter**[10] if women and men prefer doing different jobs? After all, being equal does not mean being **identical**[11].

Despite the great progress in gender equality, women still face problems such as violence, sexual harassment, and revenge attacks. Also, many women have to deal with **disrespectful**[12] male coworkers at work. Another major issue is the gender pay gap, which acts like an invisible barrier. Many women have turned to **social media**[13] to demand action. There are dozens of online **petitions**[14] about bridging the pay gap, and the list of signatures grows daily. Furthermore, the UK government recently **unveiled**[15] plans to deal with the pay gap, but it will take years to have any effect.

Gender equality is one of the biggest social issues of our time. The fight for equality of the sexes is far from over, so it's up to us to take up the cause and continue fighting.

Vocabulary

 Track-18

◆ Words for Production

1. activist (n.) 激進分子	2. spark (n.) 導火線；(靈感等的) 火花	3. gender (n.) 性別
4. be supposed to (phr.) (被認為) 應該	5. discourage (v.) 阻止；使灰心	6. obstacle (n.) 障礙
7. specifically (adv.) 專門地	8. feature (n.) 特質； (v.) 以…為特色	9. market (v.) 行銷
10. matter (v.) 有關係	11. identical (adj.) 完全相同的	12. disrespectful (adj.) 不尊重的
13. social media (n.) 社群媒體	14. petition (n.) 請願書	15. unveil (v.) 將…公諸於世

◆ Words for Recognition

outlet (n.) 表現機會	revenge (n.) 報復	invisible (adj.) 隱形的
signature (n.) 簽名	cause (n.) (為之奮鬥的) 目標	

Session 2

Watch the Video Again

> Exercise

1. According to the speaker, which of the following is **NOT** considered gender-specific for the Easy-Bake Ovens by Hasbro Company?

(A) The oven would be in colors that girls like.

(B) There used to be cute and colorful prints all over the ovens.

(C) The company later changed the oven design to cater for both sexes.

(D) The company never featured boys on the boxes or in the commercials.

9

2. What happened after McKenna Pope created her petition?

    (A) She was invited to work at Hasbro.

    (B) Her brother successfully became a chef.

    (C) She got a lot of interviews from the media.

    (D) She realized that signing her petition was a waste of time.

3. What did McKenna Pope mean when she said "Haters gonna hate"?

    (A) People just don't care.

    (B) Haters just want money and attention.

    (C) Haters are disrespectful to the activists and their families.

    (D) People should not let the haters discourage them from making a change.

4. What change would you like to make in your life? Take time to think about the question and write down your answer in the following box.

Example:

I'd like to make a change <u>to stop playing computer games too much</u>. So allow me to tell you about it.

Your answer:

_____

_____

Presentation Skill

演講者與聽眾的互動

    一般人聽演講總是在臺下扮演著被動的聽眾角色,而臺上的演講者似乎是高高在上,滔滔不絕地說著自己的故事。但這篇演講是個很好的示範,McKenna Pope 把臺上演講者和臺下聽眾的位階拉平:一位十四歲的女孩跟其他年齡相仿的聽眾一起分享她的故事。你在課堂中的演講發表也是把同學當作你的聽眾,不妨學習 McKenna Pope 的做法,拋下高高在上的負擔,把自己和聽眾放在相近的高度,拉近彼此的距離,多跟臺下的聽眾進行互動。

跟著影片一起做 / 基本步驟 (Basics)

1. **提出「修辭性問題」增加互動** 🎬 0:45-0:49 & 1:08-1:15

⇒ 「修辭性問題」(Rhetorical Questions) 指的是自己問自己問題,並不期望他人真正回答問題。例如:影片中 McKenna Pope 提到要送禮物給想當廚師的弟弟,沒有比送給他 an Easy-Bake Oven 更好的禮物了,對吧? (What better gift for a kid who wanted to be a chef than an Easy-Bake Oven. Right?) 透過修辭性問題可以引發聽眾們一致且相同的反應,用簡單易懂的問句引導聽眾進入主題。此外,修辭性問題也適用於不同主題之間的順利轉換,例如:McKenna Pope 提問 "It (the oven) would be in bright pink and purple, very gender-specific colors to females, right?",利用這個問題,她順利把主題轉換成對玩具公司 Hasbro 的不滿,因為他們設計的玩具強化了性別刻板印象 (針對「修辭性問題」的部分,本單元的第 6 點另有相關說明)。

2. **回應臺下聽眾的反應** 🎬 2:31-2:43

⇒ 看過優秀的脫口秀主持人或說相聲者,在聽眾大笑時會停下來等聽眾笑完再繼續,有經驗的演講者會隨時注意聽眾反應並做出適當回應,而非置之不理或假裝沒看到而繼續演講。影片中 McKenna Pope 說她在大約三個多禮拜的時間,就收集到四萬六千個聯署支持她的訴求。這句話引起聽眾共鳴,群起為她鼓掌表示支持,McKenna Pope 暫停她的演講,停下來接受聽眾鼓掌,並在掌聲結束後對大家說 "Thank you."。這是一個回應臺下聽眾給你反應的良好例子。

3. **邀請聽眾一起說出所要強調的重點** 🎬 4:26-4:35

⇒ McKenna Pope 認為不管你怎麼做,也永遠無法取悅網路上的那些酸民 (haters),所以她與聽眾互動,邀請大家一同說出 "Haters gonna hate.",藉此強調不必理會酸民,讓他們繼續酸下去吧,重要的是我們實際行動並做出改變。換句話說,利用這個方式成功加深聽眾印象,並強化演講者想強調的重點,帶出後續的想法及主題。

9

　　十年後的你會從事什麼樣的工作？過著怎樣的生活？你對未來的野心又是什麼呢？你將上臺發表演講，試以 "What Is My Ambition?" 爲主題，依據上述三項演講技巧，說明你對未來的野心並陳述你會採取哪些行動完成目標。

Useful Expressions:

■ (Pose a rhetorical question.) . . . Right?

■ I dream of . . .

■ Come on, say it with me. One, two, three: . . .

■ (★Share your life motto, and invite the audience to say it together with you.)

★你可以提出自己所奉行的人生格言或從下表中選一項，邀請聽衆一起說出你的人生格言 (如果句子太長，可分段念或挑重點念)。

1. "Life is not fair. Get used to it."　　　　　　　　　　　　—Bill Gates

2. "Love all, trust a few, do wrong to none."　　　　—William Shakespeare

3. "Believe you can, and you're halfway there."　　　—Theodore Roosevelt

4. "Be yourself. Everyone else is already taken."　　　　　—Oscar Wilde

5. "A journey of a thousand miles begins with a single step."　　—Lao Tzu

6. "There is no elevator to success. You have to take the stairs."

—Anonymous

7. "It's supposed to be hard. If it were easy, everyone would do it."

—Jimmy Dugan

8. "One person can make a difference, and everyone should try."

—John F. Kennedy

9. "We are what we repeatedly do. Excellence, then, is not an act, but a habit."　　　　　　　　　　　　　　　　　　　　—Aristotle

10. "Do what you feel in your heart to be right, for you'll be criticized anyway."

—Eleanor Roosevelt

Your Sentences:

1. _____
_____

2. _____
_____

3. _____
_____

更上一層樓 (Take One Step Further)

　　影片主題從弟弟想當廚師到送禮物給他，再談到玩具設計的刻板印象，最後延伸到鼓勵大家採取行動、改變現狀，成爲有行動力的人。一篇短短五分鐘的演講，進行多次主題的轉換。我們可以利用轉折語 (transitions) 連結資訊，並把所有微主題串聯在一起，達成演講想傳遞的最終極目標。

4. **利用轉折語，說明時間先後順序或步驟**

⇒ 常用來表示時間先後順序或步驟的轉折語有：first、then、next、after that、now、and so 等。單獨使用這些轉折語會有些單薄，我們可以依據上下文把這些轉折語放入句子中，更清楚告知聽衆，接下來即將引進新主題。可以參考以下例句：

(1) **Then** this got me thinking . . .

(2) **Next**, I started to realize that . . .

(3) **After that**, it reminds me of . . .

(4) **And so** allow me to tell you more about it.

5. **陳述「過去」銜接「未來」，明確勾勒主題**

⇒ 前面提到的資訊是爲了鋪陳後面想強調的重點，參考以下的例句，讓「過去」與「未來」可以順利銜接：

(1) **I've talked about** my childhood dream. **Next, I am going to tell you about** how I can realize it.

(2) **We have seen** how the air pollution endangers our lives. **Now**, **let's look at** what we can do to reduce it.

(3) **I have explained** the cooking method. **I will continue to** describe how to make my dish taste better.

9

6. 陳述事實後，利用修辭性問題做主題轉換

⇒ 影片中的修辭性問題只是很簡單地詢問 "Right?"，我們可以參考以下的例句，利用更精準的問題來增加與聽眾的互動，並順利帶入下一個主題：

(1) **I've talked about** my childhood dream. **Now, how can I** realize it?

(2) **We have seen** how the air pollution endangers our lives. **Next, what can we** do to reduce it?

(3) **I have explained** the cooking method. **But how can I** make my dish taste better?

> **Exercise**

　　延續相同主題 "What Is My Ambition?"，依據上述三項演講技巧，說明你要如何達成未來的目標。

Useful Expressions:

■ After that, I started to realize that . . .

■ I've talked about . . . Next, I am going to tell you . . .

■ I have explained . . . But how to . . .

Your Sentences:

4. _____

5. _____._____

6. _____

Your Talk

完成之前的練習後，嘗試加入本課所提到的各種互動技巧，適度地增修字句，使演講更爲完整。班級以五至七人爲一組，延續相同主題 "What Is My Ambition?"。可分組互相練習或每組派一名學生上臺演示，其他同學完成下方回饋表。

Feedback Sheet for Unit 9 — Motivating Interactions

檢視演講者的演講並據以勾選下表，給予評論，幫助其發表更精煉。

班級：_____ 組別：_____ 姓名：_____

Motivating Interactions

☐ 1. 提出「修辭性問題」增加互動。

☐ 2. 回應臺下聽眾的反應。

☐ 3. 邀請聽眾一起說出所要強調的重點。

☐ 4. 利用轉折語，說明時間先後順序或步驟。

☐ 5. 陳述「過去」銜接「未來」，明確勾勒主題。

☐ 6. 陳述事實後，利用修辭性問題做主題轉換。

Comments

NOTE

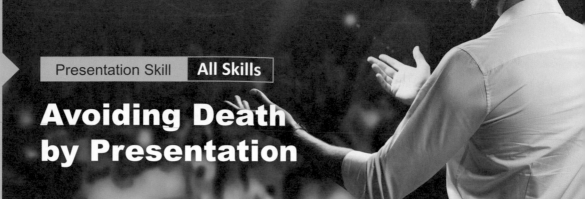

Unit 10

Avoiding Death by Presentation

Session　1

 Warm-up

When it comes to speech presentation, 4Ps are important. Read the following 4Ps and put them in the right order to help you make a good presentation.

■ **PREPARE:**

Make your slides. You can prepare a computer presentation, make charts, add the visuals, or make a poster.

■ **PLAN:**

Use a storyboard(故事解説板) like the following to plan the structure of your presentation.

STORYBOARD		
① Greeting	② Introduction	③ Main Point 1
④ Main Point 2	⑤ Main Point 3	⑥ Conclusion

■ **PERFORM:**

Speakers, use your slides to explain.
Listeners, fill in the performance evaluation sheet and give feedback.

■ **PRACTICE:**

Practice your presentation. Remember to practice your body language and think about how to **introduce**, **explain,** and **emphasize** each slide.

The right order:

Step 1: P_ _____ → Step 2: P_____ → Step 3: P_____ → Step 4: P_____

77

Watch the Video

Scan the QR code on the left to play the video.

Speaker: Sebastian Wernicke

Topic: Lies, Damned Lies and Statistics (About TED Talks)

Let's face it—nothing puts people to sleep faster than a PowerPoint. However, with some thoughts, the nightmare of a boring presentation can be avoided.

The key to selecting a topic is to know your audience. Would they rather hear something **inspiring**, or do they just want technical information? Use your own **judgment** to decide what they would find interesting. Remember, how often people check their smartphones during a talk **correlates** with how bored they are, so choose wisely!

The way you **deliver** your talk is everything. Make a **transcript** of your talk, but do not just read it out. In fact, treat it like you are talking to friends as opposed to a speech. Most people stand still during their talks, but it is imperative that you move around a little. This will help you **connect** with your audience. Choose some YouTube presentations with high **ratings** and then try reverse engineering them to figure out what makes them so interesting. For example, many good speakers start by **revealing** a shocking statistic. Some speakers add humor after making an **intellectual** point. Also, many speakers encourage the audience to think for themselves, rather than just **imposing** their thoughts on them. Of course, it is not possible to **generalize** every tip from every talk, but you can certainly learn a lot from watching the professionals.

While good delivery is essential, to give the ultimate talk, you must also make good use of visuals. Bring your **data** to life with creative animations which support your verbal **analysis**. Why not use props as well? They will make your points far more **concrete**[14] and memorable, especially if your audience is sitting through a long **session**[15].

People often joke about "Death by PowerPoint." However, the truth is, with a little effort, most presentations can be both educational and entertaining.

Vocabulary

 Track-20

◆ **Words for Production**

1. inspiring (adj.) 激勵的	2. judgment (n.) 判斷力	3. correlate (v.) 相關
4. deliver (v.) 發表	5. transcript (n.) 講稿；文字記錄	6. connect (v.) 聯結；建立關係
7. ratings (n.) 收視率	8. reveal (v.) 揭示	9. intellectual (adj.) 知性的；智力的
10. impose (v.) 把…強加於	11. generalize (v.) 歸納，概括	12. data (n.) 資料；數據
13. analysis (n.) 分析	14. concrete (adj.) 具體的	15. session (n.) 一段時間

◆ **Words for Recognition**

technical (adj.) 專業的	as opposed to (phr.) 而不是	imperative (adj.) 極重要的
reverse engineer (v.) 反推	ultimate (adj.) 最棒的	

Session 2

Watch the Video Again

Exercise

1. What are the three things Sebastian Wernicke looked at when he did the analysis of TED Talks? (複選題)

(A) Topics.　　　　　(B) Delivery.　　　　　(C) Information.

(D) Storytelling.　　　(E) The visuals.　　　　(F) Emotional impact.

10

2. According to the speaker, which of the following is likely to be a popular TED Talk?

(A) One that focuses on a project about girls, aircraft, and oxygen.

(B) One that deals with topics that we can connect with easily and deeply.

(C) One that features technical topics, such as architecture, animals, and plants.

(D) One that brings the audience to the place where they enjoy their perfect vacation.

3. According to the speaker, which of the following is **NOT** used as an example for presenters to follow?

(A) To contain false information.

(B) To pretend that you are smart.

(C) Not to cite prestigious newspapers.

(D) To provide your audience with a service.

4. What is the speaker's tone when he talked about the tedPAD?

(A) Bitter.   (B) Joking.   (C) Passive.   (D) Regretful.

 Presentation Skill

總結

前面的單元談論各個演講細節的處理，最後一個單元我們要探討演講的整體架構 (structure)。Sebastian Wernicke 的這篇演講有非常清楚完整的架構，透過這個架構，他一步步引導聽眾從引言 (introduction) 開始，進入主題 (main points)，支持論述 (supporting statements)，最後做結論 (conclusion)。他以諷刺戲謔這樣半開玩笑的方式，告訴聽眾成功演講的關鍵要素。(不過其實他同時暗示大數據雖然重要，但成功的演講並非靠數字分析就可達成目的。) 藉由這篇演講，我們可以學習如何為演講擬定完整架構。

跟著影片一起做 / 基本步驟 (Basics)

1. 擬定簡報架構

⇒ Sebastian Wernicke 的簡報架構清楚完整,大致可分爲引言、主題 (三個)、支持
論述以及結論。下圖可看出他的簡報架構:

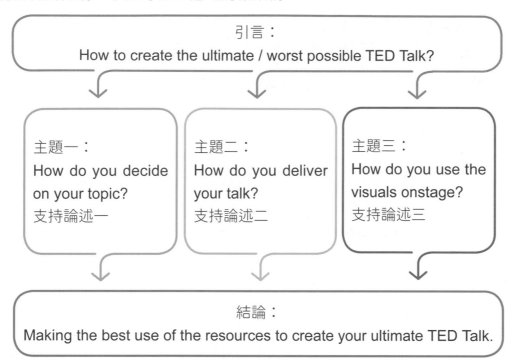

引言:
How to create the ultimate / worst possible TED Talk?

主題一:
How do you decide on your topic?
支持論述一

主題二:
How do you deliver your talk?
支持論述二

主題三:
How do you use the visuals onstage?
支持論述三

結論:
Making the best use of the resources to create your ultimate TED Talk.

2. 利用數字或例證當作主題的支持論述 　0:20–0:42

⇒ Sebastian Wernicke 用大量 TED Talks 講堂的數據,透過統計分析,得到製作成
功 (或失敗) 演講的要素。經過驗證過後的數字相當具有說服力,很適合用來支持
演講者想說服聽衆的論點。演講內容也可以試著加入新聞或網路上搜尋到的可信
數字或統計資料,增加說服力。此外,與主題相關的自身經歷或軼事來當作例子
也是演講中常見的支持論述。

10

3. 提供實用建議給聽眾 🎬 1:00–2:03

⇒ 這篇演講主旨是在分析最好或最壞 TED Talks 講堂的三大要素：主題、表達方式以及視覺輔助。在每個要素的說明後面，演講者接續提供具體實用建議，讓聽眾能更清楚地即時抓住重點並做出正確選擇。例如：挑選主題時，先說明有哪些是聽眾最喜愛 (或最不喜愛) 的主題，並提供建議，合併數個受歡迎的主題 (法式咖啡、快樂、大腦)，成為最棒的演講主題。在演講中提供具體建議給聽眾，可加深聽眾印象，並說服他們做出正確選擇。

> **補充説明** 聽一場演講的過程就像是接收實用建議的過程，從開始訓練 (training)，增加知識 (knowledge)，到個人發展 (development) 並增進技能 (skills)，最後完成自己的目標 (goals)。

Exercise

　　辦活動有可能是一項令人傷透腦筋的事，但如果能做好事前規劃及組織，活動辦成功不僅可帶給自身成就感，也可以讓一起參與的人從中獲得樂趣。你將上臺發表演講，試以 "How to Organize a Successful _____ Party / Event / Year-end Performance" 為主題，依據上述三項演講技巧，談論如何組織規劃一項活動。

Useful Expressions:

- An analysis / A study shows . . .
- It is imperative that you . . .

Topic: How to Organize a Successful _____ Party / Event / Year-end Performance

Your Sentences:

　　先依據下方格式擬定簡報架構，再參考上方 "Useful Expressions" 的字詞寫出兩句話。

1. 擬定簡報架構：

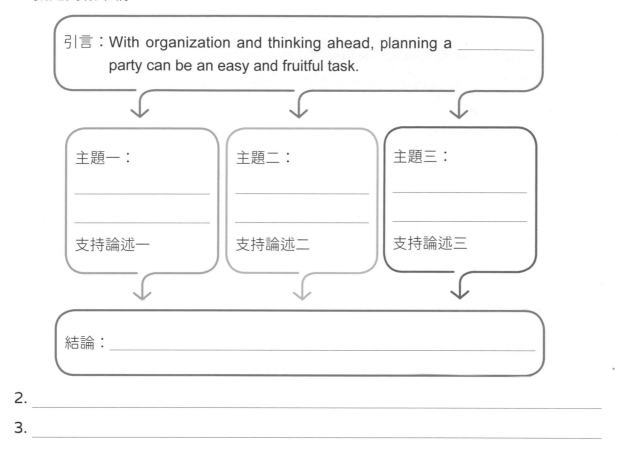

引言：With organization and thinking ahead, planning a _____ party can be an easy and fruitful task.

主題一：

_____

_____

支持論述一

主題二：

_____

_____

支持論述二

主題三：

_____

_____

支持論述三

結論：_____

2. _____

3. _____

更上一層樓 (Take One Step Further)

4. 確認演講架構三要素：引言、主體以及結論

⇒ 剛開始準備演講時，可以藉由擬定演講架構確保你能有效並清楚傳達訊息。引言 (introduction) 的功能在取得聽眾注意力，並引導他們預覽你的演講重點；主體 (body) 則呈現數個重點，並提供充分數字或例證來說服聽眾；結論 (conclusion) 則要把握最後機會，把重要訊息再次傳遞給聽眾。

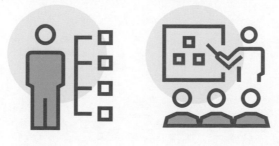

5. 使用正確時態

⇒ 一般來說，引言大多使用未來式 (will, be going to, etc.)，因爲你即將引導聽衆進入重點討論。演講的主題則多使用現在簡單式 (are, is, does, etc.)。結論的部分，若提及先前提到的數字及例證時，記得要使用過去式動詞 (were, was, did, etc.)。

6. 複誦重點並提供具體建議當作演講結論

⇒ 結論並不需要加入新資料或新訊息，只要再次複誦各個主題 (也可以用不同的字詞來表達相同主題)，並強調前面提到的一些重要數字及例子，最後提供具體建議，就可以達到結論的目的，爲演講劃下完美句點。

Exercise

延續相同主題 "How to Organize a Successful _____ Party / Event / Year-end Performance"，依據上述三項技巧，全面檢視你的演講。

Useful Expressions:

- I've covered 3 points. First . . . Second . . . Lastly . . .
- Please remember . . .
- Make sure . . .

Your Sentences:

4. _____

_____

5. _____

_____

6. _____

_____

Your Talk

　　完成之前的練習後，整合本課練習所寫下的句子，適度地增修字句，使整個演講具有連貫性。班級以五至七人爲一組，延續相同主題 "How to Organize a Successful _____ Party / Event / Year-end Performance"。可分組互相練習或每組派一名學生上臺演示，其他同學完成下方回饋表。

Feedback Sheet for Unit 10 — All Skills

檢視演講者的演講並據以勾選下表，給予評論，幫助其發表更精煉。

班級：_____ 組別：_____ 姓名：_____

All Skills

☐ 1. 擬定簡報架構。

☐ 2. 利用數字或例證當作主題的支持論述。

☐ 3. 提供實用建議給聽眾。

☐ 4. 確認演講架構三要素：引言、主體以及結論。

☐ 5. 使用正確時態。

☐ 6. 複誦重點並提供具體建議當作演講結論。

Comments

NOTE

Performance Evaluation Sheet

Use the table below to evaluate your performance. This evaluation sheet can also serve as a feedback sheet for your classmates. (利用下表評估自己或同學的演講表現)

Presenter: _____   Topic: _____

Presentation Structure (演講架構)

	(Level) Lowest				Highest
1. Introduction (引言)	1	2	3	4	5
2. Body (主體)	1	2	3	4	5
3. Conclusion (結論)	1	2	3	4	5

Body Language (肢體語言)

	Lowest				Highest
4. Eye Contact (眼神接觸)	1	2	3	4	5
5. Gestures (手勢)	1	2	3	4	5
6. Voice Inflections (聲音變化)	1	2	3	4	5

Visual Aids (視覺資料)

	Lowest				Highest
7. Quality of Visuals (視覺資料的品質)	1	2	3	4	5

Others (其他)

	Lowest				Highest
8. Humor (幽默元素)	1	2	3	4	5
9. Transitions (轉折)	1	2	3	4	5
10. Interactions (互動)	1	2	3	4	5

Comments (評語)

＊此份演講評估表"Performance Evaluation Sheet"，共分成十個評分項目，每一個項目五個 level，每一個 level 兩分，總分共一百分。可依課程需求作為部分項目評估，也可用來當作整體評估。

10

Score: _____   Signature: _____

NOTE

附錄 Appendices

▶ **演講技巧清單**

Speech Opening	1. 打招呼並自我介紹。 2. 點出演講主題。 3. 表達分享此次演講的感激之意。 4. 說明激發此次演講的背後動機。
Speech Closing	5. 講述小故事回應前面的要點。 6. 重複想要聽眾記住的重點，為演講做摘要。 7. 給聽眾建議。 8. 為演講劃下句點。 9. 感謝聽眾並開放問答。
Giving Examples	1. 舉出實例，引導聽眾的思路。 2. 傳遞比較複雜或抽象的概念時，運用實例來具體化。 3. 用圖片舉例，解釋例子更容易。 4. 舉例搭配說明，能更有條理地解釋清楚。 5. 重複強調重點，加深聽眾印象。
Telling Stories	1. 提出要求或問問題，先跟聽眾互動。 2. 介紹故事的主要人物，架構故事脈絡。 3. 陳述故事想傳遞的核心價值，為演講做結尾。 4. 引導聽眾深入探索主題特質。 5. 專注於故事本身，刪除不必要的細節。 6. 撰寫提示手卡，依序串聯細節使故事流暢。
Using Effective Visuals and Sounds	1. 利用圖片傳遞資訊。 2. 運用音效加深聽眾印象。 3. 加入圖表，簡化資訊，數字明列在投影片上。 4. 分三步驟介紹圖表。 5. 簡化文字內容。

Adding Twists	1. 演講者身分的轉折。 2. 觀念的轉折。 3. 方法的轉折，提出實際可行之改善方法。 4. 生活型態的轉折。 5. 聽眾與演講者角色互換的轉折。
Adding Humor Elements	1. 有趣的對話或軼事。 2. 誇張的言語 (exaggeration)。 3. 開自己玩笑。 4. 增加幽默元素在適當的地方。 5. 笑話或軼事要簡短並連接演講的主題。 6. 神情愉悅並面帶微笑，不幽默也沒關係。
Sending the Physical Message	1. 選好位置站定，可做小範圍地走動。 2. 跟聽眾進行眼神接觸。 3. 適當而不誇張的手勢。 4. 利用手勢來表達數字及各步驟的先後順序。 5. 利用手勢來強調重點。 6. 利用手勢來表達大小、形狀等。
Voice Inflection	1. 利用文字對比，強調反差。 2. 停頓，讓聽眾集中注意力。 3. 利用句型重複強調重點。 4. 加重 (stress) 字詞的讀音做聲音變化。 5. 拉長 (stretch) 字詞的讀音做聲音變化。 6. 連音 (linking) 增加說話流暢性。
Motivating Interactions	1. 提出「修辭性問題」增加互動。 2. 回應臺下聽眾的反應。 3. 邀請聽眾一起說出所要強調的重點。 4. 利用轉折語，說明時間先後順序或步驟。 5. 陳述「過去」銜接「未來」，明確勾勒主題。 6. 陳述事實後，利用修辭性問題做主題轉換。

實戰新多益：全真模擬題本3回

SIWONSCHOOL LANGUAGE LAB ／著

戴瑜亭／譯

ETS 認證多益英語測驗專業發展工作坊講師

李海碩、張秀帆 真心推薦

本書特色

特色 1：單回成冊
揮別市面多數多益題本的厚重感，單回裝訂仿照真實測驗，提前適應答題手感。

特色 2：錯題解析
解析本提供深度講解，針對正確答案與誘答選項進行解題，全面掌握答題關鍵。

特色 3：誤答筆記
提供筆記模板，協助深入了解誤答原因，歸納出專屬於自己的學習筆記。

★試題音檔最多元★
實體光碟、線上音檔、多國口音、整回音檔、單題音檔

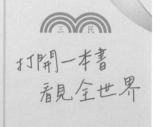

國家圖書館出版品預行編目資料

10堂課練就TED Talks演講力／溫宥基編著.－－三版
一刷.－－臺北市：三民，2024
面；　公分

ISBN 978-957-14-7722-0　（平裝）
1.演說

811.9　　　　　　　　　　　　　　112019319

10 堂課練就 TED Talks 演講力

編 著 者	溫宥基
審　　定	車昀庭
責 任 編 輯	許皓鈞
美 術 編 輯	曾昱綺

發 行 人	劉振強
出 版 者	三民書局股份有限公司
地　　址	臺北市復興北路 386 號 (復北門市) 臺北市重慶南路一段 61 號 (重南門市)
電　　話	(02)25006600
網　　址	三民網路書店 https://www.sanmin.com.tw
出 版 日 期	初版一刷 2019 年 2 月 二版三刷 2023 年 1 月 三版一刷 2024 年 1 月
書 籍 編 號	S805900
I S B N	978-957-14-7722-0

可搭配 108 課綱加深加廣選修課程

三版

10堂課練就
TED Talks
演講力

温宥基　編著
車昀庭　審定

Give a Talk the TED Way

解析本

三民書局

目次
Contents

Unit 1

Session 1

 Warm-up

1. (無標準答案，可讓學生自由分享。)

2. (無標準答案，可讓學生自由分享。)

Reading

　　在遙遠的將來，醫學科學有可能會將永生這個禮物送至人類手上。不過，到目前為止，沒有人能避免死亡。許多人寧可不去想他們有一天會死亡的事實，那想法讓他們充滿恐懼，所以他們將其逐出腦海。然而，我們如何看待我們自身的死亡——不論是何種宗教——有可能會幫助我們擁有幸福的生活，甚至有助於我們在生命走到盡頭時找到慰藉。

　　Elizabeth Kübler-Ross 在其職業生涯中，致力研究那些自知不久人世者的心理。她發現他們的反應經常依循一個模式：起初，他們發現自己無法理解這個令人痛苦的真相，於是他們否定這件事的存在。接著，他們以憤怒來回應，在最極端的案例中，甚至可能會導致暴力事件。到了下一個階段，這個人的腦中會充滿悲傷的回憶和過往的遺憾。最後一個階段則是接受死亡的事實。即將死亡的人會面對一個兩難的困境：是要繼續為生命搏鬥，或是接受他們的生命即將走到盡頭。在評估所有的選項後，他們通常會接受事實，承認自己處在即將死去的關鍵性局面。大多數的人都可以在臨終前不久的最後階段，在他們的心中找到寬恕。

　　雖然我們終將一死，但我們永遠都不應該讓對死亡的恐懼阻礙我們擁有充實的人生。如同哲學家 Immanuel Kant 所述：「一個總是擔憂丟失性命的人，永遠無法享受生命。」

Session 2

Exercise

1. He wouldn't tell them the truth because he was afraid that they would die in terror.

2. (1) A need for forgiveness.

(2) A need for remembrance.

(3) A need for the dying to know that their life had meaning.

Presentation Skill

Exercise

1. Good morning. I'm Cindy Hsu.

2. My main focus today is to share my service-learning experience with you.

3. I'm grateful for serving as a caretaker at Hang An seniors' home last summer.

4. I used to think that old people were being taken good care of by their family, but this service-learning experience changed my perspectives.

5. I've come to realize that I benefit the most from this service-learning opportunity.

6. In conclusion, service-learning can take many forms, but the purpose is to equally benefit the provider and the recipient of the service.

7. I would suggest that we spend more time with the elderly in the family.

8. That's all for my speech.

9. Thank you. We still have a few more minutes. I'd be happy to take questions from you.

Unit 2

Session 1

 Warm-up

1. (無標準答案，可讓學生自由分享。)

2. (無標準答案，可讓學生自由分享。)

Reading

　　當 Chris Sheldrick 在音樂產業工作時，他發現了一個問題。音樂家和音樂器材常常沒有辦法抵達正確的地址。於是他和一位朋友一起合作，開始重新定義地址，藉由只使用三個單字來準確定位地球上的每一個地點。

　　在一場 TED Talk 演講中，Chris Sheldrick 說到有數十億人並沒有地址。地圖上可能會顯示道路旁邊是遼闊的空地。然而，人造衛星的影像顯示，這些區域其實充滿了住宅和商家。這些地方有很大的經濟潛力，但在這些地方的人卻為沒有地址所苦。

　　Sheldrick 和他的朋友知道全球定位系統的坐標太過複雜，所以取而代之，他們把整個地球表面以三公尺見方的正方形做切割，並用四萬個單字創造三字組合，賦予每個正方形區塊一個獨一無二的地址。舉例來說，地址可以是「方塊 · 平均地 · 繁殖」或是

「著名的‧香料‧作家」。這樣的三字組合成為地球上每一個正方形區塊的辨別碼。由於讓所有人都能使用這個系統是極其重要的，所以他們也創設了不同語言的辨別碼。

取代堅持使用舊的地址系統，採用三字地址的國家會找到許多實用的應用方法。例如，三字地址的路標已分布於一些地區使用，能順利導航緊急服務機構到身陷困境者的位置。這系統可以幫助提升商業活動的效率，且會加速基礎建設的發展。簡而言之，三字地址有助於解決這些以及許多其他問題。

Session 2

Exercise

1. B   2. B   3. AC

Presentation Skill

Exercise

Topic: The Convenience of **Smartphones**

1. My smartphone brings convenience to my life, like waking me up on time every day.

2. I do many things on my smartphone for entertainment. For example, I listen to music and watch Korean dramas by using the apps on my phone.

3. As you can see from this slide, I keep track of my class hours, expenses, appointments, and more all by using the apps on my smartphone.

4. As a school student, my time is limited, so I want to have an efficient time schedule.

5. My smartphone has certainly made my life much more convenient.

Unit 3

Session 1

 Warm-up

(無標準答案，可讓學生自由分享。)

Reading

全世界的自閉症確診患者人數逐漸上升。患有自閉症的人在思考和理解周遭的世界時，會繞過一般「正常」的方式，而這正是為什麼自閉症患者缺乏社交技巧的原因。然而，這也讓一些自閉症患者擁有特殊天賦，像是非凡的記憶力。在各樣的案例中，有些自閉症患者擁有不可思議的音樂或數學天分，會讓你驚訝到說不出話來！近年來，自閉症的研究人員已發起活動來提升大眾對這個常見病症的意識。

每年的四月二日世界各地都舉行世界自閉症日。主要目標之一是要讓大眾注意到自閉症患者所面對的挫折，並試著減少對自閉症患者的偏見。希望藉由增進人們對自閉症的理解，這些無辜的患者能更獲大眾接納。

　　自閉症患者常常感到難以「融入」，因為他們不被認為是正常人，而他們的特質也被視為怪異。身為愛心社會中的一員，我們不應忽視自閉症患者的需求。事實上，我們應該要想辦法幫助他們發揮潛能。

　　隨著自閉症的比例日漸增加，顯然我們都有責任共同追求這項具挑戰性的目標。無論你的政治、文化或宗教背景為何，在世界自閉症日這一天，想想自己如何能為此盡一份心力。要無條件地接受這些自閉症患者也許不容易，但我們至少能試著作出一些犧牲，來接納他們成為社會中的一分子。

Session 2

Exercise

1. C　2. D　3. (無標準答案，可讓學生自由分享。)

Presentation Skill

Exercise

Topic: What I've Learned from **Jolin Tsai**

1. Today I have one request. Think again if you think all fans are blind and crazy.

2. I'd like to introduce you to Jolin Tsai, who is referred to as "Asian Madonna."

3. I recall the things the superstar has taught me, and I realize that I admire her for the effort she made.

4. (1) If you take a closer look at this superstar, you'll appreciate how much she has struggled to win all the praise and awards.

   (2) She reinvents both her music and image in a way that most singers cannot.

   (3) Facing criticism, Jolin thanks haters for their attacks making her stronger.

6. 提示手卡：

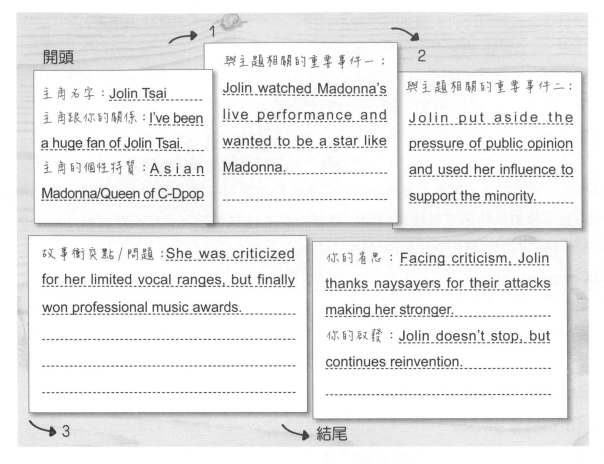

開頭

主角名字：Jolin Tsai
主角跟你的關係：I've been a huge fan of Jolin Tsai.
主角的個性特質：Asian Madonna/Queen of C-Dpop

1

與主題相關的重要事件一：
Jolin watched Madonna's live performance and wanted to be a star like Madonna.

2

與主題相關的重要事件二：
Jolin put aside the pressure of public opinion and used her influence to support the minority.

故事衝突點/問題：She was criticized for her limited vocal ranges, but finally won professional music awards.

你的省思：Facing criticism, Jolin thanks naysayers for their attacks making her stronger.
你的啟發：Jolin doesn't stop, but continues reinvention.

3

結尾

Unit 4

Session 1

 Warm-up

(無標準答案，可讓學生自由分享。)

Reading

　　我們生活在一個沉浸於聲音裡的環境，在這不斷變化的音景中，我們的日常生活皆要倚賴耳朵的幫助。因此，很難想像沒有聲音的生活會是什麼樣子。

　　對大多數的人來說，生活中沒有聲音是很可怕的。再者，從微波爐的叮聲響，到辨認他人的聲音，我們聽到的聲音提供給我們有用的訊息。

　　聲音顯然與溝通和信號傳輸有所連結，不過，它也以其他方式在我們的生活中扮演重要的角色。例如，想想音樂如何大幅改變一個人的情緒。音樂進入到我們的意識，幫助心靈釋放任何被壓抑的負面感受。聲音也可以導致行為上的改變，包括不恰當的行為。研究顯示，在吵雜的辦公室中，較難處理有關認知的工作。噪音顯然會影響工作者的生產效率，而且也會對生活品質產生巨大的影響。住在吵鬧的鄰居隔壁肯定會影響心理健康。幸運的是，聆聽符合期望的聲音是有幫助的。舉例來說，像浪花拍打海灘這種寧靜的聲音很能使人平靜，甚至有助於避免受到壓力的有害影響。令人感到寬慰的是，某些聲音也具有正向的生理影響，像是降低血壓。

給我們的聽覺一點掌聲吧。你只有一對耳朵，所以要好好照顧它們。但願它們在你步入老年時依舊功能健全！

Session 2

Exercise

1. D   2. C   3. (1) D   (2) B   (3) A   (4) C

Presentation Skill

Exercise

1. This is a picture of me taken when I went to my grandma's house for summer vacation. It was a beach near my grandma's house.

2. We used to play at the beach, listening to the waves and people's laughter in the distance. (以浪濤聲和笑聲搭配照片)

   That was really my best childhood memory.

(照片僅供參考)

4. (1) These two pie charts describe how teenagers manage their time in Years 1990 and 2018 respectively.

   (2) These different colors show how many hours each day these teenagers spent on various activities, such as going to school, watching TV, sleeping, and so on.

   (3) The key point is that you'll see how teenagers spend their spare time differently in 1990 and 2018 if you compare these two pie charts.

Unit 5

👤📖 Warm-up

Picture 1: This used to be a clean beach with fresh air. Now, it is destroyed by piles of litter and plastic waste.

Picture 2: It's everybody's responsibility to sort the garbage so that we may help with environmental protection.

Reading

塑膠汙染是每個人都應加以關切的事情。主要的問題是我們對塑膠瓶的熱愛。全世界每分鐘有一百萬個塑膠瓶售出,其中只有百分之七被回收,剩下的則是被掩埋或焚化,抑或是進入海洋。

一旦進到了海洋,所有那些用過即丟的塑膠會被困在海洋環流中 —— 海洋環流就是循環的洋流 —— 因而造成大量成片聚集的塑膠垃圾。這些塑膠會緩慢地碎裂成小塊的碎片。海洋生物吃了這些塑膠碎片,其中所含的毒素最後會進到人類的食物鏈中。

但有什麼替代方案可以取代塑膠呢?要避免使用塑膠,最簡單的方式就是使用其他材料所製的瓶子或容器。玻璃和不鏽鋼即為最顯而易見的選項。除此之外,有一些新措施和建議被提出來以解決塑膠汙染危機。塑膠汙染聯盟相信減量、再利用、回收這樣的3R 並不夠。他們的目標是提升人們對第四個 R 的意識:拒絕。如果我們拒絕購買塑膠包裝的產品,才能產生更多對環境無害包裝的需求。

塑膠汙染對我們整個星球的健全是一項嚴重的威脅。科技的確能幫助海洋擺脫塑膠。然而,如果我們打算找到一個長遠的解決辦法,那就沒有比消費者選擇更強大的工具了。讓你的聲音被聽見,向塑膠說不。

Session 2

Exercise

Do's   1. D   2. E   3. B   4. F

Don'ts   1. H   2. A   3. C   4. G

Presentation Skill

Exercise

1. I am a high school student, and I'm also an environmental protection volunteer.

2. You pay for your bottled water and quench your thirst fast. You don't think twice

about it. But, what is the reality behind that?

3.

   (1) Refusing single-use plastic bottles.

   (2) Carrying a glass or stainless-steel bottle.

   (3) Changing my lifestyle for the environment.

4. I used to look down on those who carry glass bottles, but now I'd rather carry one for the benefit of the environment.

5. This is a problem that we've created, and we can solve it. Whenever possible, we can choose alternatives by carrying glass bottles and take public transportation.

Unit 6

Session 1

Warm-up

1. Fewer than 24 hours. I usually take two showers a day when it is hot in summer.

2. Water, soap, a towel, and a shower cap are necessary when I take a shower.

3. Maybe we can use a kind of chemical lotion on our skin and rub it off to take off the dirt.

Reading

　　許多發明的出現是因為需要解決某個問題。醫學歷史上就充滿了這樣的例子，像是抗感染藥物的發明。舉例來說，抗生素拯救了數百萬人的生命。有時候，發明物最後比發明者所想像的，在更多方面幫助了人們。

　　2007 年的一個大熱天裡，一位名叫 Ludwick Marishane 的南非青少年正在和朋友一起玩，那位朋友說：「為什麼沒有人發明一種只要塗在皮膚上，就可以不用洗澡的東西呢？」Ludwick 覺得這是個有趣的想法。他試著想出了一種可以讓人擦在皮膚上的乳液，用來作為沐浴的替代品。在只有手機和網路，沒有任何其他資源的狀況下，他做了很多研究，終於發明出一種真正有用的配方。他將他的產品取名為「乾洗澡」並獲得專利。他的下一個難題是如何行銷。這名年輕的創業者知道，欣賞其便利性的有錢人會對他的產品有需求。然而，他了解這個產品對於衛生設備不夠完善的地區也會很有幫助。對那些難以取得乾淨水源的人來說，乾洗澡簡直就是救星。根據統計，一種叫砂眼的疾病影響了非洲三億五千萬人，還讓數百萬的人幾乎永久失明。但其實只要維持臉部的清潔就可以預防這種疾病。此外，每一包乾洗澡可以省下大約八十公升的水。

自從開始販賣乾洗澡，路迪克的生意就蓬勃發展。如今他的公司供應產品給來自世界各國的顧客，包括像是聯合國的這種跨國客戶。

Session 2

Exercise

1. D　2. C

3. 以下有趣的發明 (interesting inventions) 可供參考：

(1) Potato Chips

George Crum worked as a chef in New York in 1853. One day, a customer complained to him that the potatoes were too soggy. He then came up with an idea to slice them thin, dropped them into the deep frying pan and covered them with salt. To everyone's surprise, the new potatoes tasted great and successfully won customers' heart. Thus, potato chips were born.

(2) Microwave

Percy Spencer was a navy radar expert in 1945. One day when he was working in front of an active radar set, he found that the chocolate bar in his pocket melted. He started to investigate the phenomenon and experimented with different foods, including popcorn kernels and eggs. Then he created the first microwave oven.

還有更多意外的發明，可參考網站：

https://list25.com/25-accidental-inventions-that-changed-the-world/

Scan the QR code on the right for further information.

Presentation Skill

Exercise

Topic: An Interesting Story About **Myself**

1. I was wondering why they all burst out laughing the minute I finished my sentence.

2. I intended to say "30 dollars for one kilogram," but it turned out that I said, "30 kilograms for one dollar."

3. I was expecting shame and embarrassment.

4. I couldn't believe that Joe said something really nice to save me from shame and embarrassment.

5. What's the point of telling the story? Empathy and friendship.

6. Instead of making fun of me, Joe put himself in my shoes and stood up for me like a real friend.

Unit 7

Session 1

📖 Warm-up

2. Recently, whale watching has become a form of tourism around the world.

3. Humpbacks and blue whales are capable of traveling thousands of miles without feeding.

4. Although whales can remain under water for a long time, they must breathe air regularly.

Reading

　　鯨魚是動物王國中的神祕巨人。鯨魚曾經被視為怪獸而讓人畏懼，現在則因牠們驚人的體型和優雅而受到讚賞。更重要的是，近日研究發現鯨魚對海洋的健全是不可或缺的。

　　大家都知道藍鯨是體型最大的動物。然而，較鮮為人知的是，鯨魚在生態系統中扮演了不少重要的角色。信不信由你，鯨魚的糞便很重要，因為它在碳循環中具有很大的功能性。鯨魚即使死了也對海洋棲息地的穩定性有所貢獻。鯨魚的屍體為許多物種提供了如「島嶼」般的棲地，而其身體組織則為海洋食物網提供了必要的養分。

　　鯨魚長久以來因牠們的骨頭、肉和油而被獵捕。在現代，捕鯨人使許多品種的鯨魚數量急劇減少。鯨魚也面對各種來自人類活動的威脅。汙染對鯨魚尤其有害，而鯨魚也會被大型魚網纏住。考量到這些瀕危動物對海洋和整個星球的重要性，人們已發起不少國際活動來保育鯨魚。國際捕鯨委員會成立的目的在於推廣鯨魚保育，避免牠們被獵捕至絕種。國際捕鯨委員會在 1986 年禁止捕鯨，但並非所有的國家都同意停止這項活動。而且，科學研究用途的捕鯨行為仍是被允許的，原住民文化也仍可使用傳統方法獵捕遷徙的鯨魚。

　　鯨魚值得被尊重和保護。營利性捕鯨人破壞鯨魚族群或許能為某些人提供短期利潤。然而，要是鯨魚絕種了，牠們將永遠無法被取代。藉由照顧這些優雅的海洋哺乳動物，我們可以幫忙保護世界的海洋，進而保護整個星球。

Session 2

Exercise

1. B　2. ACD　3. BD

Presentation Skill

Topic: Why Should We Care About **Others**?

1. We should care about others because at one point in life, we might be "the other people."

2. By taking care of them, we are showing our love and generosity as humans.

3. If we want to ensure happiness, we must learn to help one another to accomplish this goal.

4. I have three reasons why we should care about other people.

5. The key point is that we find happiness by taking care of others.

6. It only takes you this little time to smile at someone who looks sad and say hello to him or her.

Unit 8

Session 1

 Warm-up

1. The Nazis.

2. He wanted to encourage people to speak up for the oppressed (受壓迫者).

Reading

　　每個人都有目睹過不好的事發生在別人身上,像是交通意外,或是朋友沉溺於在同學背後說一些難聽的閒話。你曾經認真思考過為什麼大多數的人在這種狀況下選擇不採取任何行動或不表達任何意見嗎?要回答這個問題並不容易,不過幸好當時機來臨時,我們都有行動的力量。採取行動及發表意見的原則在現今世界中格外重要。

　　現代社會正面對許多挑戰:仇恨言論、霸凌、暴力、種族間緊張的關係以及特權等,這還只是其中的一些。這些議題以各種方式顯現,甚至很可能會導致戰爭和種族滅絕。在日常生活中,你可能會遭遇到令人難受、不安的狀況,你會寧願不要被牽扯在內。當有人吸毒,你決定忽視才是你最安全的選擇。當你看到有人在店裡偷東西,那也不是你的問題。但重點來了:你的沉默現在也是問題之一。

　　當然,勇敢發聲可能很困難。你自然會害怕後果,也就是別人對你的批判或是嘲笑。但那樣的恐懼會在心中留下殘渣,緩慢侵蝕著你的尊嚴。試著站在被害者的角度想想吧。難道你不會希望有人可以為你挺身而出嗎?你當然會希望!每天有太多人面對仇恨和歧視。如果你可以勇敢發聲來做出改變，你還會寧願保持沉默而羞愧萬分嗎？你在良心上過得去嗎？

為正義發聲需要勇氣，但沒有人需要獨自面對這場戰役。想像一個有更多人自覺地聲援他人的社會。讓我們在該挺身而出時勇敢發聲，一起探究能讓這個世界更平等相待的方法。

Session 2

Exercise

1. B   2. A

3. I've kept silent about the fact that my family members are so used to using plastic straws. I've decided to speak up and make a change for the environment.

Presentation Skill

Exercise

Topic: The Danger of **Bullying**

1. In the end, we will remember not the wound of those who are bullied, but the violence of those who bully.

2. (pause) What if (pause) violence is later repeated by those who had a history of being bullied?

3. Bullying is depression. Bullying is anxiety. It is physical violence. It is suicide risk.

4. Kids who bully are more likely to get into fights and drop out of school.

5. Every situation is different. In some cases, kids are both bullied and bully others.

6. Bullying is linked to many negative outcomes in our lives, including ill mental health, depression, and suicide.

Unit 9

Session 1

 Warm-up

1. (無標準答案，可讓學生自由分享。)

2. (無標準答案，可讓學生自由分享。)

3. CD (答案僅供參考，不同地區及文化可能有不同答案。)

Reading

　　一百多年來，女權激進分子一直在努力爭取平等。他們的努力為引發女權運動的導火線。然而，要達到真正的性別平等，還有很多的工作需要努力。

　　在過去，女性被認為應該要待在家裡。雖然有些女性在商業公司工作，但所做的大多是傳統的「女性」職務，像是祕書和女工。此外，她們不被鼓勵做醫生和飛行員這類「男性」的工作。1970 年代，女性終於可以同時擁有家庭和事業，這給了她們表現創造力的機會。今日，女性面對的障礙比較少。儘管如此，即使是在擁有性別平等專門政策的芬蘭，大部分的護士還是女性，而大多數的工程師也還是男性。也許，男人和女人只是根據男性和女性大腦的生理特質來選擇不同的職業。但這很可能也與男性和女性行銷自己的方式有關係。不過到頭來，女性和男性是否偏好從事不同的工作真的有關係嗎？畢竟，平等並不表示完全相同。

　　儘管在性別平等上有極大進步，女性仍然要面對像是暴力、性騷擾和報復攻擊等問題。此外，許多女性在工作場合中還得應付不尊重她們的男性同僚。另一個重大問題是性別上的差別薪資待遇，像是一道隱形的障礙。許多女性轉而在社群媒體上要求採取行動。有關弭平薪資差異的線上請願書非常多，而所獲得的簽名每天都在增加。此外，英國政府最近公布了解決薪資差異的計畫，但還要數年的時間才能看到成效。

　　性別平等是我們這個時代最大的社會議題之一。追求性別平等的抗爭離結束還很遙遠，所以我們要著眼於這個目標並繼續奮鬥。

Session 2

Exercise

1. C　2. C　3. D

4. I'd like to make a change to stop studying for nothing. So allow me to tell you about it.

Presentation Skill

Exercise

1. We all want to do something that's worthwhile. Right?

2. I dream of being an inspiring teacher and the only reason behind that was my elementary school teacher, Ms. Lin.

3. My life motto is "One person can make a difference." Come on, say it with me. One, two, three: "One person can make a difference, and everyone should try."

4. After that, I started to realize that I couldn't have done this without Ms. Lin's timely

help.

5. I've talked about my dream job. Next, I am going to tell you how I can realize my dream.

6. I have explained the requirements for being a teacher. But how to meet all these requirements?

Unit 10

Warm-up

Step 1: P**LAN** → Step 2: P**REPARE** → Step 3: P**RACTICE** → Step 4: P**ERFORM**

Reading

　　讓我們實話實說吧——沒有什麼比投影片簡報更能讓人快速入睡了。不過，只要花點心思，無聊簡報這樣的惡夢是可以被避免的。

　　選擇主題的關鍵是要了解你的聽眾。他們是想聽激勵人心的內容，或是只是想吸收專業知識呢？用你自己的判斷力來決定他們會覺得什麼樣的內容有趣。要記得，在一場演講中，人們多常看他們的手機，和他們感到無聊的程度相關，所以要做明智的選擇！

　　你發表演講的方式決定一切。為你的演講擬一個講稿，但不要只是照著念。事實上，要把它當作像和朋友說話，而不是演講。大多數的人發表演講時都站著不動，但稍微四處移動是極重要的，這會幫助你和你的聽眾產生聯結。挑一些 YouTube 上收視率很高的演講影片，然後試著反推思考他們是如何讓演講如此有趣。舉例來說，許多優秀的演講者會在開頭揭示一個驚人的統計數據。有些演講者在說明了一個知性的論點之後，會加入一點幽默。此外，許多演講者會鼓勵聽眾思考，而不是只顧著把自己的想法強加給聽眾。當然，不可能從每個演講中都能歸納出各種訣竅，但你一定可以藉由觀摩這些專家而學到很多。

　　雖然良好的發表方式是不可或缺的，不過為了要發表最棒的演講，你還必須好好利用視覺效果。用有創意的動畫輔助口頭分析來讓你的資料更生動活潑。何不也使用道具呢？它們會讓你的論點更加具體且令人難忘，特別是如果你的聽眾已經坐了一段很長的時間。

　　人們經常拿「簡報常犯的致命錯誤」開玩笑。然而，事實上，只要費點心力，大多數的發表演講可以既具教育性又有趣。

Exercise

1. ABE   2. B   3. A   4. B

Presentation Skill

Exercise

Topic: How to Organize a Successful **Class Reunion** Party

1.

引　言：With organization and thinking ahead, planning a **class reunion** party can be an easy and fruitful task.

主題一：
Set your goals.
支持論述一

主題二：
Set a time and place.
支持論述二

主題三：
Organize fun activities.
支持論述三

結論：**Follow the above-mentioned steps, and you will be able to organize a rewarding class reunion party.**

2. A study shows class reunions are a great way to catch up with old friends.

3. It is imperative that you have some party games and activities to break the ice.

4. I've covered 3 points. First, I told you about how you set your goals. Second, I told you about how to set a time and place, which is the most important thing when it comes to a party. Lastly, I told you about organizing fun activities.

5. Please remember your goal for the class reunion party is to relive the old memories.

6. Make sure you prepare a draft schedule of the activities in the event.

掌握 TED Talks 演講祕訣，上臺演講不再是一件難事。

本書是專為課堂教學使用所設計的英文演講學習教材，共有 10 堂不同的主題及演講教學課程，一步一步帶領你，練就 TED Talks 演講力。

★ **為你精心挑選的演講主題**
全書共 10 個主題，別出心裁的主題設計，帶出不同的學習重點，並聘請專業的外籍作者編寫每一課主題的文章，讓你輕鬆融入 TED Talks 演講主題。

★ **為你培養敏銳的英文聽力**
每堂課的課文和單字皆由專業的外籍錄音員錄製，提升你的英文聽力真功夫。

★ **為你條列重要的演講技巧**
10 堂英文演講課，搭配精采的 10 個 TED Talks 演講影片，傳授最實用的演講技巧，並精準呈現演講可使用的常用句型，讓你成為眾所矚目的焦點，風靡全場。

★ **為你探討多元的關鍵議題**
涵蓋豐富多元的議題教育融入課程，包括生命、資訊、人權、環境、科技、海洋、品德等多項重要議題，讓你增廣見聞，多方面涉獵不同領域的演講題材。

★ **為你增強必備的實用單字**
每篇課文從所搭配的 TED Talks 演講影片精選出多個實用單字，強化你的單字庫。

★ **為你設計即時的實戰演練**
現學現做練習題，以循序漸進、由淺入深的教學引導，將每一堂課所有的演講技巧串聯並整合即完成一場英文演講，創造屬於自己的舞臺，練就完美的演講力。

※附電子朗讀音檔，使用教學請參見第I頁。

「10堂課練就TED Talks演講力」
與「解析本」不分售
31-80590G